THE
SERPENT'S SCEPTER

ELIJAH F. JOHNSON

Table of Contents

Chapter-1 : Fire!   1

Chapter-2 : Injury, Safety, Recovery   3

Chapter-3 : A Secret   8

Chapter-4 : The Learning   12

Chapter-5 : Dreaming   15

Chapter-6 : Accidental Baptism   18

Chapter-7 : The Rhino Ride   24

Chapter-8 : Pfen   27

Chapter-9 : The Listener   36

Chapter-10 : The Return   39

Chapter-11 : The Outcast of The Seas   41

Chapter-12 : The Gel Shows   49

Chapter-13 : Gone   55

Chapter-14 : The Scepter of David   58

Chapter-15 : The Hunt   63

Chapter-16 : Found   66

Chapter-17 : Captured   73

Chapter-18 : Rescue   79

Chapter-19 : Hurt and Still Hurting   84

Chapter-20 : Shot In a Café   88

Chapter-21 : Taking Action   93

Chapter-22 : Hero   110

Chapter-23 : Leader   112

To my family, for helping me with every step, to my church, for guiding me in prayer, for Ian's mom, and Ian, and to my GOD, for giving me strength... Enjoy

1
FIRE!

KEVIN BUCKHEIMER WOKE up greeted by ghastly fumes of smoke. *Smoke?* he thought. He leapt out of bed, unable to see through a cloudy mist.

"Mom? Dad?" he called out into nothingness. "MOM! DAD!" he began to panic because they always answered the first time, "Where are you?" his voice had risen, it was edgier. He ran across the room, he pulled a flashlight from one of the drawers and flipped the switch on. It lit the way a bit, but he still couldn't see very clearly. He remembered that if the door was hot not to open it. Gripping his flashlight tighter he walked towards the door, wooden planks crashing in the background. He felt the door. Warm, but not hot. He opened the door and a rush of steaming smoke poured into the room. He stepped out of his room and ran. He ran like never before, through halls up a flight of stairs and around flames. Running into his mother and father's room he screamed again, "MOM! DAD!" A sheet moved slightly, but then Kevin heard the window tear open, then fall onto the floor in a loud crash.

"Anyone in here?" a deep, yet raspy male voice called from the opening of the window.

"Um," he began, then in a louder, clearer voice "Help! My mother and father are in here!"

"Come on out boy and we'll get them after." The voice called to Kevin. He hesitated, wondering whether he should leave his parents or not. The door made a loud groan and moan, then fell off its hinges with a resounding *BOOM!*

"Hurry kid! Jump!" Flames danced into the room, creating a fear in Kevin, a fear he had never before experienced, great fear. His parents were going to die and he knew it. Tears filled his eyes then spilled out of them, waterfalls streaming out of deep blue caves. In tears, he ran to his parent's bed, planting himself firmly (well, not completely firmly) on their bed, prepared to die with them. But, he never did. He could feel his breath constricting, all of the air being sucked out, and he was clawing for air, but he could feel something else. It was two strong hands grappled the sides of his body and picked him up pulling him through the window to safety. Before he drifted into unconsciousness he felt his head slap against the window, a fiery burning in his chest, warm, then hot, then a burning sensation so intense, he lost control and began to convulse, and then he went numb. The source of the pain was radiating from his left arm, where he felt a pinch, as if two fangs had been sunk into that arm. Then Kevin's vision went black...

2

Injury, Safety, Recovery

"*IT'S A BIRD* on fire!" a civilian shouted.

"NO! Anyone can see it's a boy. ON FIRE!" roared a lady who happened to be standing by. It was true. A figure plummeted out of the upstairs window of the three-story house. It was Kevin. Then another figure emerged from the flames, just before fire engulfed the house and the two parents inside of it, then the roof of the house collapsed, sending a pillar of smoke into the air, Kevin's parents forever gone. The large figure plummeted toward Kevin and scooped him into his grasp. The flames that had been on Kevin had begun to recede from Kevin, almost magically. The man hit the ground and Kevin lay on top of him. Rolling off Kevin lay on the ground and began to fight for consciousness regaining and losing it. He could hear someone talking as he fought to stay awake, stay alive. The words he heard were "broken leg… fatal injuries … chance of death." Then he stopped breathing, only momentarily, but he stopped breathing. The doctors didn't know what it was, stress? Anguish? Injuries? They couldn't wrap it around their finger. The doctors were pumping air into him to no affect. No matter what they tried, they couldn't heal him. Until one night he nearly lost his life. He stopped breathing, but the doctors were not going to let him die. They couldn't and wouldn't. Ignoring what the machines said the doctors worked day and night until a spark lit. The next day Kevin began to slowly breathe. And after a month the flames of life had ignited and were becoming a huge forest fire of life. He began to attempt to walk and fell. They had to give him a suitable amount of stitches and surgery to keep him intact. They also had to keep him asleep in order to pry out slivers of charred wood from various body parts. On his left arm though, was where the most damage had been dealt. The arm was swollen and purple, yellow pus curled on the outsides. It hung uselessly and limply and smelled of rotting fish. The doctors believed that he had had two pieces of wood stuck there for there were two deep holes in the very center of his arm. Although they searched, they could find nothing, except droplets of unidentified venom. There was no sign of where it had come from though, because if it was truly a snakebite, they could not identify the species even with a professional. But he defied death as if it were a small bug left behind to be squashed later.

His recuperation was slow and he was happy where he was. Until he healed. Then he had to go. And go he would. But not without a fight. He kicked and screamed not only to stay at the hospital but for his mother and father. He wanted them more than anything. His life was full of ups and downs. Too much for a twelve year old. Too much. And in that moment was when the decided to stick him with a tranquilizer needle. And he drifted, away from all of the turmoil, from all of the pain, and sadness, and into bliss, where none of that existed.

"Kevin, you're an orphan. I am sorry to say this, and there is no easy way to tell you, but your parents are dead, and they're never coming back. We have tried to contact your family members, but it seems they are gone too. You're going to an orphanage." The man was tall, with sandy hair and cold blue eyes. Kevin didn't care, he simply could recall from the rest of the things that were jumbled in his mind. He didn't understand, it was a mystery to him. He could register a few things. His arm hurt, his chest throbbed, but not with actual pain, it emotions. A dark cavern had been opened in his soul, and he could find no purchase, no way of assuring himself that it was okay. Mom, with her sweet smile, and Dad with his rough hands, Kevin would never feel his mother's warmth, or his fathers embrace, he would always, and forever be alone. Nothing mattered. He was a shell, simply a fraction of what he used to be. He had no relatives. Where would he go? *Throw me out. Kill me.* Kevin didn't care what happened to him. Nothing mattered.

"We will have to send you to an orphanage. It's not too far, a mile or two away. Good day Kevin." The man stood up and walked out of the room. Kevin stayed in his chair. The policemen next to him grabbed his arms and shoved him out of the room. Kevin said nothing, he felt nothing as his face hit the wall, and the warm metallic taste of blood filled his mouth. He was nothing. He was nobody. Kevin Buckheimer was a shell.

The next day, Kevin was staring out of a car window, inhaling the scene. But he couldn't. Something, one thing got his attention. The one thing that got his attention was where he was going. An orphanage. He was going to an orphanage. His parents were gone and he was going to an orphanage. He searched his pockets, looking for all that he had.

Inside, he found the flashlight he had used, and a charred, burnt piece of wood nothing else, nothing to remember his parents by. He shoved the flashlight into his pockets. Tears welled up in his eyes, he was unable to stop them, and they poured out onto his empty lap.

He thought of something happy, but he couldn't. All he could think of was why he was going to an orphanage.

After an hour they had arrived at the orphanage. Sally, the car driver stepped out, her brown hair gleaming in the warm sun. Kevin stared at her, his legs pained and unable to do anything. She then opened the door of the car and Kevin limped out the door. He stared at the orphanage, hoping it would be a happy sight. Unfortunately, the orphanage was just the opposite. It was almost like a castle, the hulking size created a scary shadow, chilling Kevin's bones. He counted four buildings, but knew there would be more. A sign at the front of the orphanage read:

Companion orphanage

"Here we are, Kevin. Home sweet home."

Yeah, right. Kevin thought. The front of the orphanage was adorned with all sorts of stone animal faces, lions, tigers, leopards, birds and all sorts of sea creatures. He looked around and then stared at the door. It creaked open slightly and then shut closed. Sally walked towards it and knocked slowly on the hard wood. The door opened, revealing an old lady. She was shriveled, wearing a large buttoned dress that draped over her legs.

"Hello…" she looked towards Sally.

"Sally."

"Sally. Who is this child may I ask?" she asked, followed by a forced smile.

"He's Kevin, the new orphan."

"Oh. Come along. Don't want to be standing here under the hot sun."

Kevin finally noticed that he was hot. Sweltering even.

"Goodbye Sally." Kevin said in almost a whisper. Kevin slowly and unhappily limped into the orphanage, following the lady.

The inside of the orphanage was nothing of what he expected. The walls were painted a jubilant red, and the corners were bordered with gold. On each wall there was a painting of an animal. He stared at each of the paintings, mystified by the beauty. He stared at the woman next to him. She glanced at him, and as if in response to his gawking over the walls she said,

"These walls were painted by the orphanage artist."

"The artist paints very well." Kevin decided to drop the subject, but then another thought entered his mind. *Mom, Dad.* He pinched himself to avoid tears and turned to the woman next to him, expecting an answer.

"You will live a good life here. For sure."

They walked on for a while. And talked. Until they made it to the bedrooms. Once onto the second floor, she dropped him in a room labeled: KEVIN B. he went in and she told him, "In about fifteen minutes come for lunch. Six o'clock is dinnertime. Sit at table forty-nine and tell the kids Ms. Prince sent you." And with that she closed the door.

Kevin looked around the room to settle down and take his mind off of things. The room was about the size of a grown-up's room and was nice. A twin bed sat in the left corner and there was a door too. An enormous drawer for clothes lay beside the bed and that was it.

He sat on the bed, fiddled with his fingers and wept. His mother wasn't coming back and neither was his father. He wanted more than anything to be with them. It wasn't their time and to Kevin it wasn't fair. He sobbed for the next five minutes then he calmed himself down. They were in a better circumstance than he was- it was his fault that they didn't make it. Why couldn't he save them or tell the man that his parents would come first? He kicked the drawer next to him repeatedly, yelling in frustration and crying and screaming his lungs out. A small alarm clock that he did not notice before rang loudly. He walked over towards it and it appeared to have an animal that he could not recognize slung over it, sculpted in gold.

He picked it up and took a long hard stare at it. The animal he could tell had fur. Long sharp fangs jutted out of a snarling mouth. The paws had four razor claws that curved but weren't long. The clock said twelve o'clock pm. He threw it on the ground in frustration, and walked out of his room.

Kevin stepped out of his room, then was interrupted by a loud roar, one that echoed through the halls, and shook him to the core. As soon as he heard it, he hastily jumped back into the room, and slammed the door shut. As he began to breath, he crossed his arms, and slid to the ground, burying his head in his arms. *Here, of all places.*

In the lunch hall Ms. Prince awaited the arrival of Kevin. For the entire time she waited, but no one came through the oak doors. Even worse the children were noisier than normal after she had told them about a new orphan.

"Treat him kindly and be nice to him. You all knew how you felt when you first got here. Treat him how you were treated." An agreement of human and animal shouts followed…

3

A Secret

KEVIN KNEW SOMETHING was up the second he heard the roar of whatever it was. He snuck out of his room and walked down the hall. He walked across the hall, his eyes flickering around, searching for signs of those kids and he made his way towards someone's room. The plaque read JAKEY M. he opened the door and peered in.

"Hoo, hoo, hoo." Two large yellow eyes stared him down. Kevin quickly slammed the door shut. He pressed his ear to the door. Footsteps. Human footsteps. The door was opened to reveal a small boy, a little taller than Kevin.

"What are you doing? Its past lunch and everyone is supposed to be in their rooms or outside." The boy stared hard at him, his deep red-colored irises bored in to Kevin, they scared him.

"Come in." he began to open the door. " Wait." He halfway closed the door and said in a hushed voice, "Howlin get in the closet." He opened the door fully. "You're the new kid right?"

Kevin nodded slowly. Footsteps sounded from the halls.

"Get in! Quickly!" the boy said. Kevin needed no encouragement. He rushed into the room and fell on a feather-covered floor. This room was just like his room in every way except the alarm clock. This one had the face of an animal with a flat round face, with two great circular yellow eyes. On the upper corners of its face there were small tufts that stuck out and looked almost like miniature horns to Kevin.

"What's the point of this?" Kevin asked, regarding the feathers sticking to his skin.

"Ah, you see it's from my-"

"Jakey, we need you in the cafeteria. Bring Howlin." Jakey walked into his closet. The voice came from a thin girl who wore ripped jeans and a pink t-shirt. She had long, black hair that fell down her shoulders. He saw a small flicker of movement near her arm and then he focused his eyes on the spot. A low growl came from where he had been looking. He fell back in fear. Jakey appeared out of the closet with a magnificent animal latched upon his shoulder. Its face was round and its body's dark brownish hue resembled the bark of a tree. Two large round yellow eyes peered at him. Covered in feathers, this animal was very large. Great yellow feet stretched out of the lower part of the animal ending in long black talons. Kevin stared agape at the fascinating creature. It seemed just like the one on the alarm clock. Jakey and the girl left the room, but before they did, Jakey said,

"Leave whenever you feel, just don't steal anything." and the door slowly closed behind them. He sat in the room and still continued to think about that flash of color. It was certainly not the pale white color of her skin, so then what was it? He continued to think, glued to the very spot that the feathers had stuck to him until it became unbearable. He had to know what it was. He slowly crept out of the room and began to walk across the hallway; the only noise the soft *tip, tap,* of his bare feet.

Meanwhile, Jakey, his animal and the girl along with another shadowy other animal continued their walk through the halls.

"You think I should have left him there, Sadie? What if he decides to roam the halls?"

"I'm almost sure he won't. He just seems scared." She paused, only momentarily, and then changed the subject. "What do you think his companion will be?"

"Probably a deer. He seems as alert and careful as one."

"I was more thinking among the lines of jaguar. He keeps to himself and almost never seems to speak."

"Well we're here, about ten minutes late but we should be able to listen to most of the speech."

But the speech had already begun and in the ten minutes a lot had happened. Ms. Prince stood at a large podium and was attempting to quiet down the children.

"Settle down!" the children continued being noisy and obnoxious. A great roar came from behind her and everyone was silent. "Thank you Aurorua. Now that I have your attention I would like to begin the announcements. First of all, something has been sickening many of the companions and six in total have had to go to Haven." A quick murmur of the children began only to be quieted by a growl from Aurorua.

Sadie and Jakey stepped into the assembly room and they were greeted by a great pandemonium.

"Keep to the back." Sadie whispered. They all did so and crept along the backside of the wall. *ROAR!* Aurorua bellowed. The children went quiet and sat down.

"I want a quiet assembly! Tomorrow, and the next day, there will be no time to go back to your rooms, and socialize with your companions, you will study books, no training, and you will continue to do so, two days at a time until our assembly behavior improves. And if anyone lets the new orphan see one of your companions before I talk to him, we will have a tournament in the forest, survival Rebirth. Dismissed." She and Aurorua walked away through a door in the wall behind the podium, leaving the children to groan in frustration, and be escorted by the teachers to their rooms.

Kevin was there to hear the last sentence from Ms. Prince, and he knew there was something up.

He walked backwards right when the door began to open and was caught up in a rush of overly loud children.

Once the stampede had receded, he jumped to his feet, back aching and ran, seeing the faint outline of the animal he had seen earlier. As he sprinted down the halls, Ms. Prince's features coming into view. She was walking out of a concealed entrance in the wall. Behind her was a large, muscular panther almost the size of Kevin. The deep-set yellow eyes locked on Kevin and a roar sounded from it before it leaped at him, toppling him like a bowling pin. While he was on the ground, Ms. Prince walked over to him.

"Off, Aurorua." The panther nimbly leapt off in obedience.

"I'm sorry Kevin, she thought you were an Extinct." Kevin stood up to face the shriveled figure. He stepped back, ready to run away, but was stopped by the deep growl of Aurorua.

"Why?"

"Why what?" Ms. Prince inquired.

"Why? *You ask me why?* Well, Why is this panther with you? And, why is it that every single person I see has some type of animal with them? That's *why.*" Kevin was unsure of his feelings. Flustered- yes, annoyed-most certainly, scared- definitely, but amazed and happy didn't describe his mood.

"I can explain it somewhere else. Come to my room."

And with that said, they slowly walked into the secret door, Aurorua stalking behind them...

4
The Learning

"*SETTLE DOWN, GET* a seat." Kevin sat down on a furnished red chair embezzled in gold fabric. Ms. Prince sat across from him in a deep brown chair, Aurorua dozing lightly under the chair.

"Now, it all began back in the time of King David. While he ran from his pursuers, he wrote a Psalm. It was Psalm 55, if I remember. Now, somewhere in there (55:13) it said 'but it is you, my companion, my close friend.' The story was that David was out in the desert and he was running from his enemies. While he had thrown them off of his trail, a wolf by the name of Pfenolus saved him. Pfenolus was a generous silver blue wolf whose family had died. It was rumored that if you saw him, you could see the stars in his pelt at night. He was also the only silver blue wolf in the world. Well, anyway, David was taken into the care of Pfenolus. Then David realized that Pfenolus could speak to him. He-"

"Why didn't he notice that Pfenolus could talk when he was saved?" Kevin inquired.

"Well, it was because he was dehydrated and sick, so he didn't think it true. He believed he was in heaven! Although he wasn't. This was the first companionship ever. Companionship is when two beings: a human and an animal are born as one. During that time that they are in the womb, they split, and the animal transfers to an animal of its species. The easiest way to find your animal is to find its personality."

"What? Find the animal's personality? That's-"

Kevin was quickly silenced by a deep growl from Aurorua. He was trying, attempting to make her feel stupid so that he could prove that it was fake, that people didn't have animals as lifelong friends, that they didn't bond for life, but the facts were grinning at Kevin, taunting him, making *him* a fool.

"As I was saying: the easiest way to find your animal is by its personality. It's not a problem if you find your personality and compare it to animal personalities." Before Kevin could ask a new question, Ms. Prince had interrupted him and said,

"Some examples are: say you had an eagle as a companion, you would be strong, athletic and your personality would make you out to be smart and bold. If your companion were a jackal you would be skinny, medium sized, cunning and tricky. Once you have your companion, you can hear other companions, just as your animal can understand other humans. Before that, you cannot hear an animal at all. Now, continuing the story, Pfenolus saved David, helpless and nearly dead, but there was something special about him. Not only was he the root of companionship, but also he was the first and supposed last Listener. A Listener was someone who could not only hear their companion and other companions, but the Listener could hear all animals. And the Listener's companion was a shape shifter. David and Pfenolus were called the 'Duo.' Their line continued and stopped at king Zedekiah, which is why there are no more Duos. Zedekiah's mistake brought the Extincts into play. The Extincts were people that originated in Babylon. Zedekiah was a unique man because he and his companion were one. Zedekiah could shape-shift and listen to animals instead of just listen to animals. Well, anyway, the Babylonians too had companions. But these were not animals. Have you heard of the story of king Nebuchadnezzar?"

"No." And Kevin didn't care who Neba-what's-his-name was. He just wanted to go to sleep, and when he woke up, he would find that it would be a dream, fake and that his Mom and Dad would be smiling at him in the morning, arms outstretched. But he knew, Kevin Buckheimer knew that it wasn't possible, what he had just thought. He knew his parents were dead and that he wouldn't be able to sleep, and now, it wouldn't be easy. He wouldn't sleep. Not with the fact that they were gone. Kevin simply looked up, in order to stop the impending tears that welled up in his head.

Ms. Prince sighed. "Well then, Nebuchadnezzar was the king of

Babylon at the time; and every day, he forced everyone to bow down and worship a golden image. It was about ninety feet tall and towered over everyone. This image was Nebuchadnezzar's companion. Zedekiah used his power for evil though, and he divided his allegiances. He was not only bound to Babylon but he was also bound to Egypt. Before this, when he heard of the treachery that Jerusalem was committing, Nebuchadnezzar ordered to attack the province of Jerusalem. While Jerusalem was attacked, Zedekiah snuck away with a party of guards and his two sons. They were caught and his sons died and he had his eyes poked out by Nebuchadnezzar. Nebuchadnezzar became wild and ferocious and soon died. But his spirit didn't. He inhabited another human's body and swore vengeance for Zedekiah had escaped in the form of a bug. His exact words were 'Zedekiah, you and all of your animals will die.' The Extincts lived on and so did the Preservatives who we are. The Extincts got their name because Zedekiah is already dead, so the second part must be finished. The Extincts have enhanced their 'companions'. Instead of inanimate statues, they have something called a Gel. The Gels are things made scientifically which are chewed up and spat onto a statue. The gel mixes with the person's DNA and when spat onto the statue comes it has the same personality as the person. So here at the orphanage is where we take in future Preservatives. We take in orphaned kids and train them to defend themselves against the Extincts."

" So I have a companion?" Kevin asked.

"Yes you do." Ms. Prince answered, and then paused. " I believe that you should be going to your room now." Kevin walked out of the secret door and the door vanished behind him in the black hall. In darkness, he made his way to his room where he was enveloped by both his covers and sleep. Kevin looked out his window at the stars, and promised he would make up for his parents' deaths, he would do them well. Kevin smiled and closed his eyes. He was learning…

5
Dreaming

KEVIN WAS BACK in the fire. The very sight of it froze him in fear. He was paralyzed and he stood there for a few moments. His heart pounded in his chest, a rhythmic *bump, bump*. The boards crashed around him and all he could do was nimbly dance away from them. He began to slowly make his way to his parents' room. He knew that Ms. Prince had just been a dream, something fake that he had just made up. He wiped tears from his eyes. He could save them this time. A light brightened in him and he began to make his way closer and closer. Stepping with hope and purpose, he made it in and his Mom got up from the bed.

"Kevin-" her words were cut short when she was crushed by a board and she spoke no more.

"MOM! MOM!" He was awake, "MOM!" *It's just a dream. Just a dream. Just a-.* He fell back into his bed and slept again.

He was now in a grassy field overlooking a beautiful meadow. In the center of the meadow, a large man dressed in gold robes and fair hair stood there.

"Dad!" Kevin shouted in delight. Spreading out his arms, Kevin's dad hugged him and picked him up. Kevin could feel warmth radiating from his father.

"Dad it's you! I knew you were alive!"

"It is me, but I'm not alive. I am in your dream in spirit. I am here to warn you with a decree from The Creator: Kevin, be careful. A dark force rises and tempts like The Evil one from the beginning. It will tempt you and unless you resist, you will die. That's why I am sending you a message. You and your companion will be different from the rest. You two will be the D-"

Kevin's dad was cut short when a huge beast, a man of flame jumped out and crushed his father under a thick pile of burning boards.

"Dad! Dad! No! Dad, you can't." Kevin wailed loudly, teas streaming from his cobalt eyes. Seeing his parents die again was more than he could bear. It was too much, too much for a twelve year old.

"He can't what? He can't be dead?" the beast said, a hint of mockery in his voice. Kevin sobbed sadly in silence, the meadow darkening and then he was asleep. Just asleep. No dreams. No fires. No fathers. No flaming creatures. Just sleep.

The next morning, Kevin awoke and changed into a new set of clothes after taking a shower. He stepped out of his room in army pants, a white shirt and white Converses. The clock in the room had said that it was eight o'clock and it was time for school. He walked towards Jakey's room and knocked on the door. The small boy opened the door and Kevin walked in.

"So, how are you?" Jakey asked.

"Better," Kevin replied.

"You look sleepy."

"You have no idea. Bad dreams all night. I couldn't sleep."

"About your parents? I had those when I first got here. I was a baby and my parents had been assassinated by an, a..." Jakey faltered. Tears filled his eyes.

"An Extinct? I learned all about it all last night. I was in Ms. Prince's room. I might visit again."

"What was your dream about?" Jakey asked, changing the subject. Kevin told Jakey everything, from the house to the meadow. By the end Jakey had something to say.

A grim look clouded his bony features, then he smiled.

"I'm just kidding, I have no idea what that means. Dude you looked so weird for a second. Lighten up, man." Jakey looked at his watch, and said, "Oh, Kevin we should go, classes start in five minutes."

6

Accidental Baptism

KEVIN LOVED TO see the church next to his window. Every few days, when he couldn't do anything, not even homework, he would look out the window and see people getting baptized. The first time he saw it, he wanted to get baptized himself, but he couldn't ever get up the nerve to sign up. On his second week at Companion Orphanage, Kevin got baptized. Though it was accidental. That Friday morning Kevin did what he usually did: took a shower, got dressed and went to school (the orphanage home-schooled so he didn't walk very far). In the morning he had math, then he went to literacy, next came gym. After that everyone had lunch break. While they waited, many kids went to their rooms to socialize with their companions. Since Kevin didn't have one, he would just stay with Jakey. He soon learned the name of Jakey's companion. The owl's name was Howlin, and his attitude was off the charts. That was Kevin and Jakey's regular schedule. A few hours later the real schooling began. From 4:30 pm to dinner, every child had to bring their companions to Bonding School. Bonding School was when each child was trained by an older Preservative to protect themselves and their companion by using their specialties. This was necessary because a few times a year, the kids got to go to an actual battle between Preservative's and Extincts and they had to know how to defend themselves in case a stray Extinct decided to attack the group. Kevin couldn't do that because he didn't have a companion. Even though he couldn't, Kevin was given martial arts training and was always done before everyone else, so when he finished, he would watch Jakey and Howlin train. Jakey was a sloppy mess and couldn't get any thing right, so watching Jakey and Howlin was like watching a comedy show. In one drill Howlin and Jakey would close in on both sides and

Howlin would block out the opponent with thrashing wings and Jakey would come from the back and smash the neck with his wooden knife. It was simple enough, but Jakey would end up running up and the person would turn around, grab Jakey's arm and flip him over his head. After they had finished Bonding School, they would have lunch, and then do social activities (which included going outside for fun). Right now, Kevin and Jakey with Howlin perched on his shoulder walked towards the lunchroom.

The man knew his job. He would get in, sneak into the boy's room and would kill him. *Master's orders* he thought, his little Gel snake writhing in his pocket. *Get there before the boy, before the boy.* He was at the church. Walking closer and closer he quickly grabbed something out of his backpack. It was a grappling hook. He would use it to kill the boy. No questions asked. He began to swing it until he felt it was time to release and released. It swung to the correct window, landing exactly where he wanted it to land. After tugging it to make sure it was firmly stuck, he began to climb towards the window, slowly making his way up towards the room.

Kevin and Jakey had arrived at the cafeteria and were now helping themselves to their dinner. Kevin had chosen his food: some spaghetti, an apple and apple juice. He sat down next to Jakey, with Howlin on his shoulder, and across from the two was Sadie. Sadie was a skinny girl, with straight black hair; instead of curly as she had had it the first time Kevin had met her. Today she was wearing a light blue t-shirt and ripped jean shorts. Kevin, Jakey and Sadie had come to be friends, but Sadie's room wasn't very close to the other their rooms. Her companion was a white tiger named Benji. The creature was tall, almost as tall as Kevin. Kevin and Jakey usually found Sadie riding Benji. *Wow, she must be light, Kevin would think. I wonder if my companion will be big enough for me to ride it.*

The man made it into the room and crawled inside. The room was a mess! There were textbooks thrown everywhere, with an unmade bed and when the man made it to the bathroom, he wished he hadn't. It looked as if a hurricane had gone through and just stayed. There were combs and toothbrushes strewn across the wet floor and the shower curtain was open. Two towels had been draped along the door and there were bits of lotion splattered messily across the floor. *Good the boy isn't here yet.* The man thought. He went over towards the front door and peeked out. The boy was walking across the hall.

After a well-deserved dinner, Kevin, Jakey and Sadie went to their rooms. After the last good bye, Kevin walked over to his room. Once he had unlocked the door and was in, a hand was pressed against his mouth immediately. Kevin squirmed and grunted and attempted to scream but the hand was pressed firmly on him.

"Shut up or I'll kill you now," the voice whispered. Kevin obediently sat and was silent. "Now, Spargatus, come out." The snake slithered out of the man's pocket. Kevin could see molded skin that looked like scales, the snake was nearly transparent, and so it looked black on the man's sweater *A Gel!* Kevin thought. The snake slithered up his arm and sharply bit Kevin on his neck. The bite gave him almost as much pain as it had when he fell off his bike when he was eight. Kevin cried out in pain as the snake continued to bite him in various spots, poisoning Kevin everywhere it stung. The snake soon came to the two holes that had healed in Kevin's left arm. They were closed, but ruptures and veins still wriggled beneath his skin. The creature bit down and the holes were reopened, the fangs fitting perfectly. Blood squirted every which way from Kevin's arm. He cried out in agony and then the blood hit his face, flecks of venom sizzling and popping on his bare cheeks. He screeched, yelping and struggling to wipe off the evil venom from his cheek. After the sixth bite Kevin couldn't take it. He had to get away. This was when his martial arts kicked in. The man had loosened his grip, seeing Kevin getting weaker and weaker, so Kevin took advantage of that and twisted his right arm behind him, grabbed a comb and smacked the man's funny bone so hard the man toppled backwards. Kevin flicked the snake off and it flew onto his bed, bouncing into the trash basket. Kevin was up now and so was the man. Kevin took a weak stance, his arms low and then the man struck. He blindsided Kevin, striking a sucker punch that landed on Kevin's face. Kevin fell back and landed on the ground. The man attempted to pick Kevin up, but Kevin twisted around quickly, his arm out and his hand in a fist. The fist slammed into the man's face and he flew backwards, falling onto the ground. Kevin ran out towards the door only to find it jammed. Kevin rushed towards the open window and nearly screamed, "Help!" but two hands pushed him out with enough forced to propel him out the window and he began a plummet towards the baptism water outside.

Father Peter was a nice man, a little round, but he was kind to all. Dressed in his regular outfit, a large golden robe adorned with a thin red scarf, he half walked and half wobbled wherever he went. Today he was performing baptisms and it was eight at night at the time. The church service had ended and everyone was leaving before he said: "let us say this: for this baby," he said, picking up a small baby. "As a church, my young one, we, the church baptize you in the name of the father the son and the holy spirit. Now."

"We the church baptize you in the name of the Father, the Son and the Holy Spirit." At the same moment, Kevin hit the water and the church had begun the words. When it was over someone said to father Peter,

"Father, was that a splash?"

"I do not know." He said, in his Father-know-it-all voice which was high pitched and snooty. He said, intrigued, his curiosity getting the better of him. "Let's go check it out." They both walked over to the baptism pool and found a bloody form in the water. He began to panic and screamed a blood-curling scream that the killer heard.

I have to get out of here the killer thought while looking through the window down at the dead boy. He walked out of the room and went down the hall. He soon found what he was looking for. A teacher. All alone. He slowly crept up behind her until she stepped into her room. He followed, and punched her in the face, which knocked her out cold. Then he took the teacher's uniform, a white coat with a CO patching on the left. He put it on and took out his snake, which slithered into a small hole in the wall. The man walked out of the room and made it to the front door. He had killed, got away and completed his mission.

About twenty minutes after he was found, Ms. Prince took Kevin to the hospital. On the car ride, Aurorua had licked the blood off of Kevin's arms, legs and head. The rest was drenched in blood that continued to spill.

"Snake bite." Aurorua hissed to her companion.

"Was it a Gel or a snake? Either way, we have to get him to a hospital, Haven is too far away." Ms. Prince said.

"It was both. It wasn't an unformed gel or a regular snake. It was a Gel snake."

"Oh, God. And we don't know whether it had venom or not."

"Then put the petal to the metal old woman and step on it!" Aurorua screeched.

"Fine then. I'll show you the old woman." Ms. Prince muttered angrily, and stomped her foot on the pedal. The entire car shot forward, Aurorua flying into the trunk and Kevin spilling into the trunk after the panther.

"STOP! STOP!" Aurorua screamed in agony as the boy's limp body crushed her. The car finally stopped and then Ms. Prince got out, walked to the trunk and opened it up. There was Aurorua, with Kevin's body across the floor of the trunk.

"I managed to get him off of me." Aurorua gasped. She nudged him into Ms. Prince's open arms and Ms. Prince closed the trunk door after saying, "Stay, okay?" then walked away and into the hospital emergency room.

Ms. Prince began to change posture, going from formal to tired and sad "Help! Help! I need someone to take him!" she screamed, letting as much tears fall as she could. A nurse ran over to get Kevin and bombarded Ms. Prince with questions.

"What's his name? How did this happen? Where? How long ago? What did this?"

Ms. Prince answered all of the questions.

"His name is Kevin, he was bitten by a circus snake and the snake was sent to be put down immediately. Because of all the venom, I think he fell out of his window, which is why we found him in the baptism pool down below. And it happened about a half an hour ago." Only about half of what Ms. Prince said was true but the nurse didn't question anything.

"And what sort of relation do the two of you have?" the nurse questioned.

"I'm his grandma." Ms. Prince lied.

"And what's his last name?"

"I can't give you that." Was the answer.

"Okay. The boy will have to stay here for a week, because we believe it was a poisonous snake."

"Okay."

The next day, the nurse went to bring the medicine to the room and she was humming along towards the lobby, to pass by the old woman, but the old lady wasn't there. *Humph, some grandma.* the nurse thought. As she stepped onto the elevator, she thought, *Maybe the grandma's with the boy. It was probably Jim who let her in.* She stepped off the elevator and thought her theory was right. When she went in, she dropped the tray of antibiotics and screamed. The window was open; the bed a mess and worst of all, Kevin was gone…

7

The Rhino Ride

KEVIN WAS AWAKE. Ms. Prince had taken him after seeing one or two Extincts among the staff. When Kevin had asked her what was going on, the answer was:

"To find your companion." Kevin had been delighted and was silent for the ride, taking mental guesses about his companion. Next to him, Aurorua would speak to him and tell him it would be okay and that after this he would never be hurt again. Once they had made it, Kevin saw his first warrior Preservative. The man's hair was deep brown and his jaw was thick and strong. His arms were bulging in muscles and he wore army cargo pants and a white muscle shirt. At his side was a huge white rhino.

"So it's just you two plus me?" he asked in a deep gruff voice that boomed at every word.

"Yes. Kevin this is Sergeant Grant and he is going to give us a ride."

"Where's the car or plane?" Kevin asked. Grant laughed.

"What's so funny?" Kevin asked.

"The ride," Grant chuckled, " is right in front of you."

Kevin turned to stare at the rhino.

"His name is Thundarx. He's nice and friendly," Grant paused, gazing into the horizon. "Alright, let's get a move on, I want to get you guys there before sundown."

They hopped onto the hulking creature and Kevin asked Aurorua, "Aren't you coming?"

"I'm going to run alongside." Aurorua answered with a nod. Ms. Prince frowned at him.

"How can you understand Aurorua?" He shrugged, and she shrugged it off too. Kevin hopped onto the rhino and with a whistle from Grant; the rhino was off, Aurorua running steadily beside. There was no talking during the ride, just the rhythmic up and down beat of the rhino's running. As the day wore on, Kevin began to sleep, but at about 6:00 p.m., Ms. Prince awakened him.

"Kevin, get up! We're under attack!" Ms. Prince whispered hastily. He was in a small clearing and had been placed in a sleeping bag. To the right and left of him there were two other beds. In the center of the clearing a solitary fire blazed and provided a dim light for Kevin to see a little. Kevin looked up and couldn't see Grant or Thundarx. But in their place he could see a huge figure with a rhino's head and ripping biceps. Also, instead of hands, there were bowling ball sized hammers that were smacking away and attacking four Gels of the same size and height. The Gels had long lizard-like faces with reptilian wings in the place of arms. Rows of sharp teeth and nails jutted out of their snarling mouths. There were slits instead of eyes, red dots in the middle and in place of a nose there was a horn with two gaping holes that you could see through. Kevin couldn't see any Extincts but they could be everywhere. Kevin saw Aurorua and Ms. Prince moving closer and closer together and then they were one. In place of the two of them was a sleek woman with black fur and there was a long X in black leather across her body. The head was not the face of the gnarled Ms. Prince, but that of Aurorua. Inside of two sheaths on the back in a criss-cross were two huge blades of deep black, which were unsheathed, and brandished menacingly. Then Ms. Prince/Aurorua came for the lead Gel that had a long curved blade in its hand and a golden band around its neck. It bared its blood red teeth and the battle began. It sliced in an upper cut motion and Ms. Prince/ Aurorua dodged to the side, and then continued by slicing the blade onto the ground and sticking the other knife into the throat of the animal. The animal screeched and batted the blade away, slid underneath Ms. Prince/Aurorua and then they stabbed the Gel in the gut and released, the beast screaming a blood-curdling scream that Kevin had to plug his ears not to hear. The creature backed away and slithered into the bushes.

"Kevin, it is safe," the fused creature said. "You may call us Ajkar."

"Okay." Kevin said, his voice shaking.

"You must go now, run before they get you!"

"But I can't leave without you guys!"

"Go!" Ajkar said after dismantling and stabbing the creature that charged her. The number of Gels was growing. There were nearly forty Gels trying to get at Kevin, but Ajkar and Grant/Thundarx were pushing them back slowly. Kevin couldn't go, he had to be useful for something. Then, before he could stand up, a hand grabbed his foot. Kevin's face turned pale and he had a split second to realize what had happened before the hand began to pull him away.

"Help! He-" his next word was cut off when a hand covered his mouth and then he was looking into the face of the gold banded Gel. There were no eyes on its face and its tongue lolled open and Kevin could smell the rank breath and he could feel its claws digging into his skin, blood oozing from the damage done. It was completely black and its teeth, Kevin could see were from various animals, he could see about four shark teeth, a scorpion claw, two stingers and tons of snake teeth that were purple. It lifted a hand to give a killing blow but then a deep bark came from behind and then the Gel turned to face its opponent. The fur of the opponent shone with a silvery blue tinge, glowing with a radiance of an unseen light. There was a firm and muscular aspect to this creature, and most of all a beautiful and mystic one. The opponent was a silver blue wolf...

8
Pfen

THE WOLF SNARLED,

"This one is not for your taking." The creature let out a hiss.

"Go boy, get behind me." The wolf whispered to Kevin. Kevin began to move towards the wolf but was abruptly stopped when the creature snarled and stuck out its gnarled arm and pushed Kevin beside him.

"Give me the boy." The wolf growled through gritted teeth.

"Over my dead body." The creature's voice sounded like hundreds of snakes speaking at once, hissing and spitting simultaneously. The wolf growled angrily and charged. The creature flew into the air and then kicked the wolf to the ground in mid air, slicing the wolf across its back. The wolf fell and lay splayed there in the dirt. It got up, shook its fur and bared its teeth. This time, the creature charged. It spiraled into the air, swung around its head and spat at the wolf. The wolf dodged the spit and rolled into the leaves. Where the wolf had been and the spit had hit, there were burnt leaves and smoldering ashes. The wolf charged and leapt into the air, spinning and biting the creature on its wing. The beast screamed in agony and hit the ground. Slowly, it stood up and dove at the wolf, arms outspread, talons ready to rip. The wolf slid under the beast and raked its claws down its opponent's stomach. The creature flopped to the ground nearly lifeless and then the wolf killed it with a swift bite to the neck, crunching through bone with a sharp *crack!* The creature dropped to the ground, dead and limp. Then, it shuddered and turned to a silver-blue puddle, flecked with red blood.

"Come Kevin. We must go."

"How do you know my name?" Kevin asked, scared to see the wolf speaking to him with the silvery blood dripping from its mouth.

"I know many things that you don't. Now come."

"I have a question though."

"What is it?"

"What was that?"

"It was a Brechen."

"A—a what?"

"A Brechen. A Gel that has no Extinct. You can consider them the lowest of the ranks when it comes to the Extincts. The one's with the gold band are venomous, so if one spits at you, dodge quickly I suggest. Also, stay away from those with the ringlet of the Master." Before Kevin could ask the question, the wolf answered it, "The Master is the ruler of the Extincts. He leads and commands them. I suggest using a good thick bladed weapon when fighting these things."

"What's your name?"

"My name? It doesn't matter right now. We must go."

Kevin could hear more Brechen coming. He began to run, but the wolf stopped him.

"Get on." Kevin obediently hopped onto the wolf's back and the two charged away. Kevin now knew why Sadie was on Benji half the time they saw her. With the wind whipping behind him and the wolf, Kevin felt like he was on the top of the world. *This is great!* Kevin thought. He didn't want it to end but it did. After passing thick growth, they could no longer hear the great battle between the two grown-ups and the Brechen. They had come to a spot from which they would have to jump. A large overhang had caved in and surrounded a greatly vast pond. It was the very center that brought the true beauty. Although the light of evening had come over the pond and light had settled on the great pond, the luscious island in the middle stood out the most. Its banks were covered in thick shrubs some of which were snapped and broken. Kevin heard a loud roar and another, softer roar. The trees began to shake and then the wolf told Kevin "Go now! Run."

Kevin stood in thought for a moment.

"Where should I go?" Kevin asked. The trees began to shake closer to them. The wolf turned towards him and said, with fear in every word,

"Go to the end of the bank. You will see a fallen sapling there. It connects to the island, cross and then roll the tree into the water. You will see a pack of wolves. Tell them I sent you. Lead them into and away from here in a secret tunnel. The tunnel is near the center of the island. You will see a tree; under it is the tunnel, covered in thick leaves and shrubs. Answer the Wise Turtle's Riddles and Questions, for the Creator sends him. Then you will pass."

"What is your name?"

"My name is-" he was cut off, even though he was speaking quickly and hurriedly, by a loud roar.

"Run!" the wolf shouted. Kevin didn't have to be told twice. He tore around the perimeter of the pond, never turning back. Once he had made it the fallen sapling, he looked to the wolf. What he saw turned his blood to ice. There, in the very front of the wolf, a large tree-like form stood. It had thick leathery swamp-green skin covered in warts and bumps. The legs were massive and on the end of three toes were deep black talons, around two feet long and sharp to the point. The stomach was covered in a silvery black color, shimmering like death itself. Its arms were studded in claws and animal teeth that stuck through the skin, claws and teeth of all animals, crocodiles, snakes, sharks and others just to name a few. The arms ended in one huge saber-like sword that curved inwards. The face had the snout of a lizard and with two deep black eyes, red rimmed and furious, this creature was a death sentence to any human. But a wolf is not a human. The wolf snarled as it had when it faced the Brechen and launched itself under the giant beast. The beast, for a creature of its size, was surprisingly agile. It swept around and in one moment cleaved the wolf in two pieces. The body flopped to the ground, lifeless and dead. Kevin stared in horror, tears beginning to fill his eyes. This wolf had saved his life more than once and now, without Kevin knowing his name, had died trying. Kevin fell to the ground on his knees and wept. The creature turned and fixed its beady eyes on Kevin. Kevin heard it roar and find itself new prey. Kevin stood up and began to stumble across the sapling bridge. The creature was right on his heels, roaring and grunting with every movement. Kevin had made it to shore and was now attempting to push the sapling into the water but the creature was too heavy. He soon felt it budge and began to push it to the water. The creature was three feet away, two, one and then the sapling slipped into the water and with a final roar, the ghastly beast plunged into the depths of the murky pond. Kevin could see the last bubbles ripple on the surface of the water as the creature drew its final breath and stayed at the very bottom of the lake. Kevin now could smell something. It was smoke. *Smoke?* Kevin thought. He turned to see the trees aflame and Kevin dropped to the ground in unconsciousness.

Kevin had awoken from a sharp nip to his arm. In his face, a small furry face, with a snout, stood atop his chest and was wagging a short, stubby tail. It was a wolf pup. But something that separated it from a wolf was its coat. It was a glossy, light bluish tinged color, dappled with twinkles of bright light. *Pfenolus?* Kevin pondered.

"Hello, you're a man-pup, aren't you? What's your name? Oh, forgetting my manners. I'm Pfen. Are you going to-" the wolf pup spoke so fast he was panting, his tongue lolling out of his open mouth, drool slipping out of it. Before he could continue speaking, a larger wolf, this one with a sleek, steel gray tinge with white spotted the young one speaking to the boy.

"Pfen, get away from him, you'll disturb him while he tries to rest." The small wolf didn't stay or go, but just slunk back into the shadows. His deep pelt provided him perfect camouflage and he could not now be seen by the naked eye.

"That little rascal." The she wolf muttered. "How are you getting along?" she asked.

Kevin responded in a regular tone, used to talking animals.

"I'm fine, but I'm famished. Haven't had a bite to eat in a while."

"Our hunters, Lookan and Simber will bring a good stout deer, or if we're lucky, a moose. He was always able to hunt better than the two of them." She gazed off, looking into the distance. "Did you see my mate?" she asked. Kevin nearly said no, but he then remembered the wolf.

"Yes," he said, pausing momentarily as tears clouded his eyes. "He died saving me." The she wolf stepped back, shaking her head in disbelief.

"No, no, my mate, Pfenolus, you're coming? Right?" she asked, regarding the outside world. There was no answer. She gave a short howl of anguish, and then lay down, refusing to speak to anyone. By late afternoon, she looked at Kevin, while he roasted a thick amount of meat on a fire. It had been tedious work, for Kevin knew nothing of the outdoors or fire. He had started by rubbing two sticks furiously together to no avail. After, he had plied some charred pieces of bark and had shaved off slivers of bark, by sliding a stick across the tree's trunk. The shavings came in short curls and soon he had a handful of them. Once he had made it to the wolf den, he had come outside and had gathered sticks and put them in a shabby pile. Now came the hard part, making the fire. Kevin searched his pockets, but they were empty, so he had swum across the pond, which was a last resort, being careful that the beast didn't get him and had searched the charred trees for a fire, and after a while, he found one. It was still ablaze but contained on a tall tree, about fourteen times the size of Kevin. But this was fine because it was only in a small hollow that had caved in and bunches of leaves and sticks had fallen, kindling the fire. He snatched a fallen stick and put in to the fire. Kevin was sweating. He didn't want to do it, but he was hungry, and hunger had driven him to be as fearless as possible. But he was still deathly afraid of fire. So he sweat. And when he had finally made it back to the den, all of that hard work had paid off. Since he didn't have time to make a spit, he just held the meat above the fire until it had cooked. The she wolf said, " What were his last words to you? My mate's."

"Huh? Well, he tolth me thath he wouldn't be comin' back, and shaid that I wazsh sthposed ta bring you guysh to the Wiszze turtle." Kevin said through a mouthful of deer meat.

"The wise turtle?" the realization hit Kevin.

"We have to go! Now! Pack up! Were going!" Kevin said, snatching up hunks of deer meat, taking a stray leaf and beginning to bundle them up. The she wolf stood up and seemed to grow larger. Then, in a loud, clear voice shouted. "Nobody leaves without the permission Storma, the mate of Pfenolus!" she boomed. Kevin fell back, his fear sprouting over the edge. Storma seemed to shrink back, returning to her regular size.

"You do not move this family without my permission." She said sternly.

"Now, explain what it was that he said."

Kevin took a deep breath.

"Well, he said for me to come here, tell you guys he sent me and then lead you guys to the Wise Turtle. He told me to answer some riddles and some questions then go away to take you guys to a safer place." Kevin explained.

"Did you know his name?"

"No."

"Few do, and some who know hardly believe it. His name was Pfenolus. He was the Great Wolf."

Kevin stared at her, a blank expression on his face.

"What?" he said, still not understanding it.

"He was Pfeno-"

"I now know that, but how?"

"He was given a new life, in wait of the Listener, and now that he is gone, the Listener has come."

Kevin continued to stare, dumbfounded. Storma pressed on,

"You are the Listener, Kevin. That is why you can understand us animals. Didn't you notice it?" Kevin paused.

"Well not really, when Ms. Prince was teaching me, I didn't really pay attention very much and then-" Storma cut him off in mid-sentence.

"Shut up! If Pfenolus told you what he did, then you must go. Simber! Lookan!" she barked. Two stout looking wolves came into the scene. "Gather the pack, we move!" The two wolves ran off, shouting orders to the rest of the pack. Within minutes, a small pack of thirteen wolves was ready and at Kevin's command. There were the two hunters, Simber and Lookan, at the head of the pack with three mothers and there were six pups along with two elders. The small group shuffled without knowing where they were going along with protests of having a human leading them. Kevin agreed, for he hadn't listened completely to Pfenolus. That was another thing that Kevin couldn't understand. That wolf was Pfenolus;

the great wolf that had saved David was in his time and was alive, and yet he had been taken down so easily. Kevin didn't believe it himself, though, after four weeks, he had become accustomed to things he didn't believe but had to accept, like talking animals and evil people called Extincts and people who were specially bonded to animals. Those things he didn't believe, but had to accept and now he was accepting that the wolf was Pfenolus. He began to think, his senses reawakened when he heard a wolf, one of the elders named Wrefen.

"We *are* going in circles! I marked here not twenty minutes ago. We're going in circles, and going around and around! We should move inland, towards the center of the island, where it's warmer." *The center!* Kevin exclaimed silently. He now knew where to go thanks to the wolf.

"No, I know where to go. Thank you Wrefen." The wolf stared at him, menacing with hatred flaming in his eyes. *Poor thing, he just wants to stay at his home.* The wolf stalked away from the group, grumbling "I'm gonna catch somethin'." he left without another word into the bushes. Kevin turned to the pressing matter: getting the family to the center.

The troop of Brechen had shortened in numbers from the attack of the two Preservatives. They had gone from over one hundred fifty to about sixty-two Brechen. Their leader, called the Ochere had been killed facing Pfenolus, so his second in command had taken the golden band and become Ochere of the vicious pack. Their spy had come, sneaking through the underbrush. The spy, standing in front of him was Wrefen the wolf. Ochere fingered his teeth and was now taking a large chunk of meat between his two front teeth.

"What news do you bring me?" The creature rasped. The wolf was scared, and couldn't get much out.

"Th-the Listener is with them. You must kill them now. He leads them to the Wise Turtle." The Ochere nodded to the two guards next to him. They grabbed the wolf and shoved him towards the Ochere.

"Do you know my master's mission, wolf?"

"Yes." The wolf whimpered.

"So you know he entrusts me to kill every animal, correct?"

"Yes." The wolf began to step back, only to be prodded forward by the guards' spears.

"Along with every Preservative, right?"

"Ye-" the wolf gurgled and slumped to the ground. Ochere withdrew his blade from the wolf's neck. Wiping it on his arm, he barked to the two guards, "Get this filth out of my sight." He stood up and shouted to his troop of Brechen, "We move! I want to taste human flesh tonight!" His remaining troops stood up and formed a clumsy rank and from the nod of Ochere, they were off.

Kevin and the pack had made it to the Wise Turtle. He was a small turtle, a blue shell painted with swirls and stars. His feet had small spines that curved up and out of his ankles, making it look as if he had wings. An old and wizened face stared at Kevin.

"Is it entry you wish?" the cracked voice said.

"Yes." Kevin replied.

"Then you must answer my riddle."

"Got it."

The turtle began in a soft almost musical voice:

I am your friend, not your enemies'

I am there for you, thick and thin, straight and bend,

I will not separate from you, for if I do, I am done,

This, my friend is because we, my partner and I were once one

Kevin thought for a moment. What could it be? He sat down and turned to the right of him and went over to the pack. He told them the riddle and they all were just as flabbergasted as him. He turned to the turtle and asked,

"How does this work again?"

"I ask you the riddle, you answer. Then," he said, pointing to a small hollow filled with gnarled leaves and roots, " those open and you get away. You get one chance." The turtle then began humming softly and ignoring every word that was said. Kevin cursed.

"If only I had a companion, this would be much easier."

Storma came up to him, panting with a pained expression across her face.

"Kevin! Brechen! About sixty of them, coming fast." Kevin cursed again.

"Um, um, um." He didn't know where to start. He could now hear the heavy footfall of synchronized steps from the Brechen. They were nearly there; Kevin could see the gnarled outline of their bodies.

"If only I had a companion." Kevin continued to mutter under his breath. Storma took action quickly.

"Everyone, get the pups behind you, be ready to take these Brechen down!" the wolves snarled at the oncoming force of Brechen. They were getting closer and closer. Storma fell back, a small bundle between her teeth. She made her way towards Kevin and dropped it in his outstretched hands. The small pups at the back scattered, only to be caught by the Brechen and slain immediately.

"Kevin! You must go with Pfen! He must continue the line of Pfenolus!" Kevin bit back a protest after seeing the pain in her eyes. He nodded to the she wolf, the small wolf in his hands. And went back to solving the riddle.

"If only I had a damn companion!" He muttered for the third time, this time loudly. The walls parted, Kevin slipping through and looking back. All of the wolves lay on the ground, slain and lifeless, with their enemies' bodies scattered too. There were six Brechen left, including Ochere. Ochere turned to Kevin, seeing him staring dead at him.

"Charge!!!" he screeched. The remaining Brechen charged, only to hit a flat wall. Kevin and Pfen had made it through…

9

The Listener

KEVIN HELD THE small wolf pup in his arms, keeping the pup close to his chest. As he ran, he began to see which pup it was. The little pelt twinkling with light in the dark of the tunnel belonged to that of Pfen. It all made sense. Pfen was the son of Pfenolus! That explained the stars in his pelt. He heard a crash and then turned to see the Brechen moving towards him chanting,

"Kill! Kill! Kill!" they were gaining on the boy, moving at an astounding pace. Kevin ran as if his life depended on it, which it did. The small pup couldn't die and he couldn't either. He had to save this little scrap. He began quicken his pace, moving faster and faster until he came upon a dead end. He was stuck! He couldn't scale the wall, and the Brechen were coming. He stepped back, and fell. For he had just stepped onto a thin layer of leaves that was the way out of the death trap he was in. He fell deeper into the ground and once he hit bottom, broke into a stiff-legged run. He could see it on the other side of the tunnel. Light. The one thing that he had wanted and craved was there. He began to increase his speed, the light getting closer and closer. He ran through, into the light and turned to look around. There, in the thick shrubs, shouting, "Kevin, come here!" was Ms. Prince. She and Aurorua were separate and now Aurorua was heading for the Brechen pack, all six of the demons. She flashed her teeth, letting the bloodbath begin. She came for the first one, the rest forming around her and jabbing their spears in and out. One of them, a stupid one at that, jabbed his spear at the flaring face of Aurorua. Aurorua snatched it in her teeth and with a sharp flick of her neck, snapped the spear in half. This Brechen was armed with a large cutlass, too, and fumbled with his wings to draw his sword. It was too late when he finally drew it. Aurorua had pounced on him, sticking her claws into his neck and then, with a sickly *Surch!* the Brechen was dead. She turned to the others, baring her teeth. The Ochere stepped forward and growled although it sounded like a screech. He drew a long cutlass from his belt. While drawing it, though he cut through the belt, which flopped to the ground making him look like a complete idiot and then, since the cutlass hadn't completely come up, he sliced his waist. Ochere screeched in pain and then looked up to Aurorua to see her laughing hard along with the other four of his crew. He growled his growl and charged Aurorua, blindsiding her and knocking her to the ground. Ms. Prince stepped in. She jumped to Aurorua's side and in a swift flash of light, they were Ajkar. They drew their blades and stuck both through the chin of the Ochere, closing his mouth, the tips of the blades protruding from the spot where the nose of the Ochere should be yet there was the hollow horn. They soon made swift work of the rest. Ajkar jumped at one and knocked it to the ground, and, before it could cry out it was dead from one of the blades. Ajkar charged the other three. One fled and then Ajkar stuck the two, one to the right, another on the left. The other was at least ten yards away when Ajkar's blades sang through the air. One flew right through the back and fell to the ground after sliding through without a problem. The second embedded itself in the back of the Brechen's head. The creature fell to the ground without a sound. Ajkar withdrew the blades and ran to Kevin and Pfen, whom they had left when Ms. Prince had gone to Aurorua. Kevin who had watched them, stood there in awe with the wolf pup not even daring to look up. Ajkar soon became Ms. Prince and Aurorua again. Ms. Prince stepped towards Kevin and said,

"It has been a long time since we've had a wolf companion."

Kevin corrected her with his newfound knowledge.

"You mean it has been a long time since you've had a Listener. A long time since you've had the Duo." Kevin paused, then said,

"Actually the Duo isn't really complete because I don't have a companion yet." Ms. Prince's face was full of shock, disbelief and joy.

"Kevin, you're the Listener?" she asked.

Kevin grinned. "Yup."

"I do not believe this. How?"

"Well," Kevin told her the details of his story from when Ajkar had told him to run. Ms. Prince interrupted him while he was talking about being taken by the Brechen.

"Ooh, if I could get my hands on that Ochere then I would, I would-"

"You can't. Pfenolus killed him."

"Pfenolus?" Ms. Prince was lost, so Kevin filled her in. It grieved her to know that Pfenolus was dead. When Kevin finished, he said,

"Kevin, hold out your right arm." Kevin held it out. She turned it so that it was elbow down and pulled up his sleeve to show his skin. There, in the mid-section of his arm was a figure.

$$\alpha\chi\varpi\sigma\phi\delta\tau$$

The shape was a diamond that in the center had a compass rose of deep black, and then in an unrecognizable language it said something. The diamond's corners were a shimmery blue color, a black crescent moon holding the diamond in place. Ms. Prince read his mind.

"It says, in the Ancient Speech, the Listener. You, Kevin as the Listener first of all hold great power and second of all, have a companion already. Kevin, you're special. You have powers like no other human. You're different. You're set apart. You are a hero."

"How?" Kevin asked.

"When you first see your companion, you will feel a small nip, then you'll see your companion, as the Listener." Kevin was still confused.

Kevin looked out of Ms. Prince's jeep, inhaling the scene. His companion, Pfen lay beside him. They were headed for Companion Orphanage. Everything now made sense to Kevin. They pulled into the parking lot of the orphanage and Kevin smiled. He was home…

10
The Return

KEVIN WENT THROUGH the doors of the orphanage, smiling when he saw the red walls with the great paintings of animals. He made his way to his room only to be intercepted by Sadie, Jakey and another boy with blonde hair who was wearing a rugged outfit. The boy wore Hawaiian button-up shirt that had holes and punctures in it. His shorts were khakis that had more pockets than Kevin could count. He wore brown leather sandals and was looking at Kevin through black sunglasses. Kevin nodded to him then went to his friends.

"Kevin!" Jakey said, a smile across his face. His voice quieted

"What happened to you?" Kevin looked down at his jeans. They were in shreds and were now only classified as the poorest excuse for shorts. His skin was drenched in blood under there and it looked as if his skin was red. He had more than one puncture wound in his skin and he was hunched, as if his back ha broken. His shirt was ripped and torn, jagged and splayed in different directions. His arms were bare and his Mark was showing. When Sadie set her eyes upon the Mark, she looked up to Kevin, her expression changed. She nudged Jakey and he hadthe same reaction. Jakey nudged the boy and Kevin thought he could see shock in his eyes.

"We 'ave a great force in arr' midst." The boy said, in an uneducated accent. He looked at Kevin

"Where's ye' companion?" the boy asked. Kevin and Pfen had begun to grow in their companionship and Kevin soon found that they could communicate in their minds, being the Duo. *Pfen?* The reply came in a small voice. *Yeah, Kevin?*

Pfen, come, now.

"He's coming. I might ask you the same thing." The boy smiled, and in an explaining voice he said, " Not all companions have to be ground walkers. Mine comes from the seas." He whistled and from a small pool Kevin hadn't noticed before, Kevin could see a head larger than the Wise Turtle's but resembling it, poke out of the hole. The head was rough and leathery, white flecks dusting it. Down its face, in a curving arc was a long strip of golden skin. Kevin stared and marveled at the magnificent creature.

"Let me introduce us-" a small bark interrupted him. Pfen came in. He had grown since Kevin had first seen him and was now about one-and-a-half-feet tall, his coat glimmering in the light.

"Hello. Pfen at your service!" he yipped. The boy stifled a giggle. Kevin had found that Pfen, being part of the Duo, could transform. The downside was that he could not hold that form for long, so it did not happen too often, turning into an elephant, that is. He turned into an elephant, his skin becoming leathery and his mouth sprouting two tusks and a large trunk.

"Do you dare laugh at me?" he boomed. The boy stepped back and then apologized. The wolf pup went back to being a wolf pup and his cheery self. The boy continued, "Let me introduce us. This, moi' friends is Hawksbeak, my Leatherback turtle." He said, indicating the large navy blue turtlehead poking out of the water.

"And I, am Darren, Outcast Of The Seas at ye' service."

"Outcast of the seas?" Kevin asked. Darren looked at him, a smile crossing his face.

"Well, it all began when"…

11
The Outcast of The Seas

"*ME AN' HAWKSBEAK* 'ere were young. We would play tricks on the sea-faring men when they harbored. Idiots they were. We always used the same trick an' then, we boarded the ship. We would eat our fill and then when it was time fer' land ho; we would rob the lot o' dem'. Well, we would then 'ave me, the great thief, jump overboard and onto Hawksbeak ere'. Well, one time it went wrong. They shot me while I jumped into the sea. I got hit an' me an' Hawksbeak were lost at sea. We shored on a small island, wit' dis' ol' hermit who lived dere'. He sheltered us, wit' dis ole' turtle that was always wit' him. He taught us 'bout companions and preservatives an' the lot o' dem'. Well, we learnt bout' Extincts an' soon met em'. Dey outnummered us two ta one. Da man, Ole Jo died savin' me an' Hawksbeak ere' an' told us to go ta Companion Orphanage. We're 'ere to avenge is' death. He was like a fader ta me." Darren paused, finishing his story, trying to sound brave, but the tears streaming from his eyes gave him away. Kevin didn't get it. Darren hadn't mentioned anything about him becoming Outcast. Kevin could sense that he was hiding something. Something deep, and dark. He muttered something and then jumped into the water hole, hopping onto Hawksbeak's back and with that, they were gone, underwater and out of human sight. Kevin's eyes goggled.

"Don't worry, that's a regular thing with him." Sadie said, reassuringly. She and Jakey escorted Kevin to his room, where he changed into a new outfit. He put on a pair of army cargo pants and wore a white t-shirt. After that, they had to go to Bonding School. Kevin was separated into a different room, with three men and four women standing apart by about four feet. Ms. Prince materialized from one of her secret doorways and stepped behind Kevin.

"Kevin," she said in her soft voice, but yet it startled Kevin and he turned around, looking into her weather-beaten old face.

"Ms. Prince!" he yelped. Pfen was staring at Aurorua and questioning her while Kevin talked with Ms. Prince. The wolf was more muscular and built than he had been when Kevin met him. He was still about a foot and a half tall, but when he went up to other companions, he always seemed to grow in size.

"So Kevin," Ms. Prince asked, "are you ready to begin Bonding School?" Kevin nodded.

"Then let it begin." The first person, a woman named Alice with a small kestrel on her shoulder stepped forward. "Kevin, we will not tell you what to do. You and Pfen will have to come up with something your own way. We will arm ourselves, but with wood only, this being your first time. Let it begin." Kevin walked over to the shelf, which was arrayed in weapons ranging from a forty-pound mace to a small object that resembled a frying pan. Kevin picked up a large wooden knife that was about half the size of his arm. The weapon felt balanced in his hand, its leather handle fitting perfectly in his grip. His opponent stepped forward, kestrel hovering in the air. Pfen growled and his posture began to change. He began to shrink, his pelt turning into mottled brown and black feathers. His face flattened and his nose disappeared. In place of his front legs, wings sprouted, and his back legs turned hard and scaly, with a yellow tinge. His little claws turned to humongous talons, black and sharp. In place of a small wolf pup was a large, Great Horned Owl. Pfen shrieked and bounded into the air. He clawed at the small kestrel, but it slid under him and she stuck her foot out which tripped Pfen in mid-air. When he hit the ground, he was no longer the Great Horned Owl but was a small wolf pup again. Kevin charged the lady, seeing his companion hurt. She was holding a large sword, which even though it wasn't metal, glinted. She had a studded breastplate, too. She sidestepped Kevin and then tripped him, sticking her sword under his chin.

"Do you surrender?" she asked. Kevin paused. She pressed it tighter to his neck. Kevin turned to look at Pfen. The kestrel's sharp talons had him pinned down. Kevin nodded to the wolf pup.

"We su…" Kevin stopped, his expression becoming fiercer.   " W e never lose!" Kevin roared. He swung his sword around and slammed it into the helmet. Alice crumpled to the ground. At the same moment, Pfen had bitten one of the kestrel's legs and it had become airborne. Pfen changed form, but this time he turned into a sleek, jet-black goshawk. He leapt out and into the air, snatching the small kestrel in his talons. He held the bird in his talons, upside down. The bird went limp after Pfen slammed his head onto the wall. Kevin stepped forward fiercely.

"Who's next?" Kevin asked

The grown-ups stepped back to reveal Sadie, with Benji by her side. She was clad in a black leather jumpsuit, with crossed swords behind her back.

"Kevin, get a sword, and then we'll really fight." She said crossly. Kevin walked over to the shelf and chose a replica of his sword in a steel form. He buckled it from shoulder to waist and stepped forward. Pfen had decided to turn into Pfenolus, his father. Kevin flinched momentarily, but feeling the essence of the Great Wolf comforted him.

"Let's do this." He whispered to Pfen. They stepped forward in unison. Pfen charged Benji blindly, Benji side stepping and sticking his leg out to trip Pfen. But Pfen was ready. He turned and leapt into the air, bowling over the white tiger. They began to tussle, rolling and biting and scratching and kicking. Sadie charged Kevin, her blade striking his cheek and drawing blood. Kevin touched his cheek and looked at his fingers. They were stained red. He leapt at Sadie and she kicked him to the ground. She nearly got her blade on him, but he rolled over and sliced her leg. Kevin felt the ground moving under him. Literally. He looked down to see long blades of grass erupting from the room's once polished marble floor. Trees began to crawl through the cracks, breaking up tiles and wood. The seven grown-ups had gone and then the voice of Ms. Prince boomed through an intercom.

"Attention all students of Companion Orphanage! We are now holding our monthly tournament! You will form groups of four and then you will put on suits with large leather buttons. To win, have every other group's leather buttons slashed. I will give you guys twenty minutes to group up and arm yourselves. The winners will receive a prize of an electronic device of their choice, and gourmet dinners for the rest of the month." Sadie smiled at Kevin.

"You did well, considering you're a newbie. Come on, let's gather the rest of the team." They walked off, in search of Jakey and Darren. When they had gotten everyone, Sadie told Kevin one thing,

"Food and water first. These things usually take a long time. Then we take down the rest of them to win."

Ms. Prince's voice boomed again, *"Let the Companion Tournament begin!"* Kevin heard a mighty roar of orphans sound throughout the halls. They had named their team "Crossed Blades." They then took off, hearing loud announcements of teams getting taken out.

"'Knot it now' is out! 'Thrice as good' is gone!" Kevin and the others had made their way to a small pond, where they decided to camp. Kevin gathered sticks, and piled them up. Sadie set them up to make a fire. Night was closing in on them; the only audible sound was the chirping of crickets and incessant buzzing of mosquitoes. Kevin slapped his arm to shoo off a mosquito for the fourth time. Sadie stood, shouting commands to Darren and Jakey, who were building a hut. Jakey brought along a bed sheet knowing it could be useful, and sure enough, when he and Darren finished, they had a large hut, with a bedsheet roof that had star designs, with thick twig and stick walls that were reinforced with mud. The first to guard was Kevin. He stood outside the hut, his hand gripping the sword. He began to look around, staring at everything. There were a few berry bushes along with some poison ivy ones too. Kevin began to wonder whether he should build a wall, but then stopped when he heard the rustling of leaves. He nudged Pfen, who was dozing at his side. In Thought-Speak, (the language in the minds of the Duo), Kevin said, *Pfen, are you there? The reply shot back; Of course, I've been sleeping here. Where else could I be?*

I dunno, it's just I heard a noise in the bushes and I think it's another group.

Got it.

Pfen's form began to shrink and shrink until there was only a small form about the size of Kevin's thumb. Then, after pausing, Pfen scuttled off, not one sound being made. After a minute or two, Pfen was back. He turned back into his regular self.

There are two of them in the front, and then there's one on the right and one on the left.

Thanks, Pfen wake up Hawksbeak and I'll get the rest of them.

Kevin stepped into the hut, bleary-eyed and tired. He shook each of them awake while saying, " Get up, we're under attack."

They all stood up, drawing their weapons. Sadie had her double blades, Jakey had a knife with a small red circle separating blade from hilt and Darren had two discs that had little spikes and four little holes where he could fit his fingers through the middle of the discs. They stood up in a line shoulder-to-shoulder. Sadie began the orders.

"Darren, I want you to flank the large group and I'll hit them head on, while Kevin attacks with Pfen and me. Benji, you'll get the guy on the right and Jakey, take the one on the left."

They trudged out, eager for a battle. Kevin followed Sadie, the two of them shouting, "Crossed Blades!" The two in the front charged them, slashing and dashing. Kevin locked himself in a duel with a buff boy holding a large morning star with a bear companion. Kevin and he circled for a while, only hearing Sadie and the opponent pummel each other. Then Kevin got an opening. His opponent stumbled and began to regain himself, but Kevin was on him in a second, slashing each of the circles. He was on the last when the boy grasped him and threw him over his head. Kevin hit a tree, stumbling to regain his balance. The boy was on him, morning star swinging. He swung it, the force smashing into Kevin's chest and bowling him over. Struggling to regain his breath, Kevin staggered to his feet. The boy leapt at him. Kevin thought he would lose when he heard, "Charge!!" Darren exploded from the hill in thick scaly armor, with a hooked head that resembled a turtle, but his face was showing. The turtlehead was more of a helmet, the top propped up. On his back was a huge, round shell that was like a circle with a small cone in the center. The deep ultramarine of his armor shone while it flashed terror. Darren was getting closer, and then the guy looked up,

"What the f-"

Darren smashed into the guy and he flew at least three feet away, Darren striking roundhouse punches and head butting. Darren stepped back and threw one of his blades straight at the guy's circle. His blade hit home and struck the last circle. When Darren stepped back, the ground under his foe began to crumble and disintegrate. The boy fell into a deep pit, and then the ground closed up. Kevin let out a shriek.

"It's okay," he said, "That 'appens to 'em when they lose. They're okay, it's just so that they don't cheat and keep playing."

" Y- your voice, Darren, it's different."

" Yeah, that ole crone Ms. Prince is givin' me lessons."

" Oh, okay." Kevin heard a deep roar from behind him and screeched "Pfen!" The wolf was tussling with a massive wolverine, the creature's jaws snapping open and shut. *It must be from the girl Sadie's fighting with,* Kevin thought. Sure enough, Sadie and the girl were still attacking each other, Sadie with two circlets left and the girl with three. Kevin drew his sword to intervene for Sadie and Pfen, but Darren stopped him with his hand.

"Let them fight their own battles." Kevin watched the battles, looking back and forth, Pfen to Sadie, Sadie to Pfen. The wolverine had Pfen pinned down and then Pfen would shrink into a bug, slipping under the legs and then regaining his shape. He raked his claws across the back of the wolverine. The wolverine screeched in pain and hit the ground, the earth under him disintegrating. He turned to Sadie to see her standing over an abyss of black. Her black jumpsuit was torn in multiple places and she was badly limping on her right leg. She had one circle left. Kevin looked at his. There was one left. Jakey came back with Howlin hovering above and Benji by his side. Ms. Prince's voice boomed,

"'Flashing fire' is no longer in the tournament!"

Crossed Blades made their way back to their camp and took guard shifts and rests. At about four o'clock Sadie began orders.

"Kevin, you and Darren pair up and find at least one camp. Jakey, find something for us to eat and I'll guard camp." She stopped and thought for a moment then said, "Kevin and Darren, report to me when you get back, then." She said, speaking to everyone, "We will take the camp that Kevin and Darren find. This entire tournament is about teamwork, and our skills, how we can survive, being out in the wild." She finished and walked over to the hut, limping with a white piece of bed-sheet knotted around her thigh. She took her place and stood at the front of the hut, solitary and quiet. Jakey walked off, Howlin on his shoulder. Darren walked away too, Kevin in tow. They began to move through the undergrowth, Darren pausing to look at the ground and say, "I think I've got 'em." They found their way through the growth, navigating and moving around, always alert and on watch. When they paused, Kevin found a small raspberry bush and plucked some fruits from it, tossing a few to Darren who was on watch while they momentarily camped. As Kevin munched on a raspberry, he thought of Pfenolus. Tears streamed down his cheeks. The Great Wolf was dead thanks to him. Darren walked up to him.

"Let's move. I want to find Red Star, the team that's been winning all the time. If we find them, we'll just report back to camp and then we take their camp. After that, with a full crew we can beat Red Star and win the competition. I want to get them because they're the most dangerous team." They trudged on, Darren's gray shirt blending in with the woods. Kevin's vision began to get hazy, his thoughts wavering as he saw the same tree with the crooked shape for what he thought was the third time.

"Darren, I've seen this tree more than once."

"No, you couldn't have, it would have had an X on it from when I mark every tree we pass by."

Kevin looked at the tree and sure enough, there, in a light tan color on the rough brown mottled with gray tree was an X.

"Right here, Darren, and here, and here! You don't know where we're going, don't you?"

"I-I of course I know where to go." Darren said, flustered.

"Then where are w-" Kevin was interrupted by a loud noise in the bushes, then four kids in their leather armor charged down the hill, shouting at Kevin and Darren. They drew their weapons, and charged. Kevin blindsided the first person and the kid was on the ground out cold. Quickly slicing, Kevin had the kid in the abyss in seconds. Darren was locked in a fight with two kids, his blades flashing and slicing four circles in total. Kevin ran to intervene, but then he remembered Darren's words, *Let them fight their own battles.* He turned to the fourth kid, who was making a run for it up a hill, charging at him and shouting his war cry,

"Crossed Blades!" he bowled the kid over and then he was thrown down. The kid charged him, but Kevin slid to the side, batting his blade up in the air. It flew with the wind. It thudded ten feet away from the boy, behind Kevin. The kid's face blanched. He had two circles that were across from each other, parallel. Kevin sliced them both in half with one stroke and the kid went tumbling into an abyss. The companions had been snoozing on the top and the three remaining fell into their own holes. A boar, a squirrel and a jaguar plummeted into their own depths. Kevin made his way down the hill, hearing Ms. Prince's voice, "*'Painted Bright' is out! There are three teams left, 'Crossed Blades', 'Red Star' and 'Bears rising'. May the best team win!*" the voice ceased and Kevin could hear a group of kids charging down the slope.

"RED STAR!!" they shouted, thundering towards Kevin and Darren.

"Run!" Kevin shouted, and they were off, running against impossible odds at the mercy of the most dangerous team in the orphanage...

12
The Gel Shows

SPARGATUS WAS HUNGRY. He wanted human flesh. His Extinct had promised him the flesh of the boy, and then, they had to throw him out. From his underground cavern, he was able to catch mice and rodents. But he wanted more, he wanted human flesh. It was all he thought about, all he wanted. He had watched the boy, knowing his every step from his chain of passages that he had raided. He had grown sufficiently since he had first bitten Kevin. His long body stretched sinuously for forty feet. His head was jagged and knife-like, shining sleek and dark in the night. He was at least two feet thick and about three feet from his head there were long arms that were about as large as a human. On the end of his arms, were heavily scaled fingers that sprouted long, blue claws that shone deep like midnight. His most deadly weapons were his teeth. They were two purple fangs that jutted from his mouth, at least four feet long, and sharp. He remembered the first time he had tasted the boy's blood, had savored its taste and relished it in the middle of the fire. Then his prey got away. He knew he could taste Ancient blood in that child, but he didn't know how. And now, he was slithering through his pit, searching for a meal until he heard the voices,

"Kevin! Come on!" it was that blonde boy with the turtle, the person Spargatus hated the most. He didn't know why, he just hated him. Then he smelt *him*. The boy was nearing. Behind them, a group of kids charged toward them, swords drawn. He was angered. They could not ruin his meal! He hissed in defiance and slithered to where they would be any second from now. He heard them thunder down the hill and then he reached out his hand and snatched the leg of the kid behind the group.

She screamed and hacked at his arm, a small margay at her side nipping and biting him. He bit down on the girl and she went limp, then turned to the animal and flicked it into the darkness. He slithered into his main hall, a barely lit room that with the little bit of light that it got giving it a bluish tinge. In the very center was a large stud of rock that held a long, golden pole that was about a yard long. Four horns of silver sprouted from the end of it, royal inscriptions carved around it. Held in the grasp of the four horns that curved inward was a large circular opal that was interlaced with strips of gold. The girl gasped when she saw it and muttered something that sounded like " Supper for later" to Spargatus. He hauled her over to a long pillar of stone that supported his main cavern. Hefting her over to the massive stone column, Spargatus grabbed a long coiled rope and snapped it in half with one bite. Then he snapped the two halves in half again. Using one of the fourths, he tied the girl up. Then, he slithered out of his lair. He would eat the girl and the rest of her group. But he wanted them all together so that he would feast when the day was over. He snatched up the unconscious margay and tossed it into a blazing fire. He heard the girl scream in agony and smelled the savory smell (to him) of burnt flesh and singed hairs. He plucked the roasted wild cat from the fire and began to eat his fill. When he was done, he rose into the world. His massive form was nearly transparent, yet he radiated an Ancient Evil that could not be seen through. He stalked off, following Red Star, or what was left of them.

Kevin and Darren stumbled and blundered throughout the forest/orphanage, hoping for unexpected help. Together, they had succeeded in taking down a mountain of a boy, Darren losing his discs and then appearing with a long dagger that was thin and sharp. Darren threw it, not only slicing through the circle it targeted, but it also sliced the arm of the boy. Instead of slowing him down, it did the opposite.

"Now we've got a hungry troll coming for us." Kevin muttered angrily. Darren heard him, turned around and smiled.

"It's not every day I get a fight like this," Darren said.

Kevin turned abruptly and yelled defiantly at the large boy. Behind him, a massive gorilla bore down on Pfen. Pfen had changed into a perfect replica of Thundarx, the rhino. He charged the gorilla head on and batted it into the air, its massive hands floundering in the air. The boy charged Kevin, a large battle-axe drawn. Kevin ducked under him and flew at the boy. He landed on his back, hacking at the air. The boy flipped him over his head and onto the ground. Kevin scrambled for air as it was knocked out of him. Then he heard it.

"Charge!" there was Darren, in full turtle armor, two turtle leg shaped blades in his hands. They were bronze with deep white flecks across them. The hilts showed intricate carvings of turtles. Darren looked taller and more robust. Kevin guessed this was his and Hawksbeak's fusion.

"Hey chubs." It got the boy's attention and he looked up glaring at Darren.

"How about you take someone on your own size?"

The boy grunted and his gorilla walked towards him. Kevin had seen this process hundreds of times with Ms. Prince and Aurorua. At the end, when the flash came, it was a deep gray, almost a wind that knocked Kevin to the ground. In place of a boy and a gorilla, there was a tall, tree-like form. Brawny arms were separated from shoulders by shields of gold. A Roman helmet squeezed the pudgy face, long spikes jutting out, pointing every which way. The face was deep gray, with thick flaps of skin folding into it. Where a nose should have been, there was a slight curve with two holes in it. The eyes were small and beady, red and full of malice and hatred. A large hammer with a stud on the end was what the Gorilla/boy was armed with, encased in obsidian, making the weapon shine in the sun. It was muscular, every part of it covered in muscles and veins that popped out. It wore a small piece of animal hide to hide its unmentionables. Its feet were brawny, piles of matted fur sticking to it. It roared and blundered towards them, arms outspread with the hammer in its right hand. Darren flew through its legs and held out the blade to slash the gorilla-boy's leg. It did just that. He tripped and hit the ground, his hammer thudding twenty feet away. Darren hopped onto his back and held his sword in the air.

"Crossed Blades!"

Then, Spargatus stepped in. The boy had become human again and his gorilla stepped up and roared at Darren. All of a sudden, it stumbled and began to be pulled back by invisible hands. Spargatus crawled from his hiding place and raked his claws across the gorilla's head. The gorilla roared in pain and turned to see its adversary. It saw the glittering red eyes. It saw Spargatus bare his fangs. Horror crossed its face. It saw the Ancient Evil in Spargatus's eyes. It didn't see the death barb coming for his chest. It felt it end his life. Spargatus shoved his barb deeper and deeper, every time it went deeper, the gorilla's face contorted into a new form of pain. His stubbed barb slipped through the heart and out of the back. The gorilla slumped over, and breathed his last breath. The boy got up, hammer in his hand,

"You will die!" he shrieked. Spargatus looked at him and waved his hand as if to say, *come on, meet your death.* The boy charged him and swung his hammer. It skimmed Spargatus's cheek and then what happened next, Kevin could never say again. Spargatus came down on the boy, his fangs sinking into the boy's neck. Then, it did something that Kevin was all too familiar with. As if in some sort of trance, Spargatus began to move rhythmically, up down side to side on the boy, sinking his fangs into various places, making the boy scream in agony and then blood began to squirt out of the boy, venom sizzling and popping on the boy's bare arms and face. Then, when the boy was drenched in blood, his body slumped on the ground, Spargatus began to rip and tear at his neck and once he had finished, there was no longer a boy there. Kevin gasped after seeing the procedure.

"That's- that's him." He stepped back and shouted one word, "Run!" Darren needed no further urging. They shot away from Spargatus, the snake slithering and hissing in tow. They made their way to the camp, Spargatus right behind them.

"Run! We're under attack! Run!"

The camp began to stir. Sadie charged towards the two scouts and they reported quickly.

"Sadie there's a-"

"Big huge thing and-"

"It killed this boy and-"

"It's coming for us." Darren finished.

Sadie cursed in a very un-lady-like way. Darren raised his eyebrow.

"Jakey! Go run and tell Ms. Prince what's going on. Me and the others are going to hold this guy off."

Kevin's face paled.

"You're not going to-"

"What? Are you scared?" Sadie teased.

Kevin's face reddened.

"No. I just- I- I." Kevin glared daggers at her. "I am not scared." He growled, every word coming through clenched teeth. They turned to face their adversary, Kevin with his blade drawn, Sadie with her blades, and Darren with his imperial blades. Spargatus was gaining. Darren joked, "If I had a mom, I would be telling her I love her."

Spargatus burst into the clearing, teeth bared and arms outstretched.

"Sadie don't let him get his teeth on you." Kevin said.

"Wasn't planning on it," Sadie snapped. Kevin rushed forward and sliced at Spargatus. The snake slithered out of his reach and pushed him aside. Kevin hit the ground and stayed there after the snake slammed his head into the tree. He had just enough time to see Pfen land beside him. Everything he could see went black.

"Kevin!" Darren shouted and shot towards the serpent. He bowled it over and hurriedly stood up. He clouted the snake with one of his blades and drove the other deep into its chest. It slithered in pain and brought its claws down on Darren's head. He hit the ground and then rolled over as the snake spat its venom at him. Where he had been, there were sizzling and popping leaves. It drove its claws into the spot where Darren had been and turned to look at him. Darren had been furiously whispering to Sadie and was now making a beeline for a large oak. Spargatus zeroed in on Darren and then when it was too late, knew he had fallen into a trap. His tail flared up in pain. He turned to see the girl in black hacking at his tail. He hissed and charged at her, flicking his tail out of her reach. He swiped his arm; claws extended at her and then felt large claws ripping into his side. He turned to see the white tiger, Benji tearing at his side. Cobalt fluids oozed out of his side making him roar in pain. Then he felt a long, golden blade sink into his cheek. He ripped it out, making him wince in pain and saw a large blade, golden with white flecks and on the hilt were intricate carvings of turtles in deep blue. And stuck to the blade was a piece of paper that read,

Do You Want more? I hope not because we have an entire legion ready to shoot a few arrows at you and turn you into a porcupine.

The Serpent Scepter

Hope you give up and run, Darren Hawkback

Spargatus turned furiously to Darren and saw him smiling and waving at him, one blade in hand. Darren pointed across the clearing at a black form. He thought it was the girl again, but then he saw four new shapes and a small boy. At the lead of the group was Ajkar. Help had come.

13
Gone

"*STEP AWAY FROM* the kids." Ajkar said slowly and calmly. Standing behind her was Grant and next to him was Jakey. Along with them were two seasoned Preservatives with longswords at their hips, behind their backs quivers filled with arrows and in their hands bows with arrows strung and trained on Spargatus. Next to each of them were black otters. Spargatus turned to them, his silvery blue blood streaming from his side, cheek and tail. Sadie and Darren dragged the limp forms of Kevin and Pfen, their companions in tow. Spargatus hissed and held out his hand to stop them, but an arrow twanged into a tree three inches from his hand. His arm recoiled and the children walked across to the larger group.

"Go away." Ajkar commanded.

He hissed and then threw himself into one of his tunnels. It collapsed, and he was gone. There was a huge hole, stretching more than thirty feet across, gaping at them, its dark depths covered by mist. Kevin gasped and stood up. Darren was by his side, tense and quiet.

"Guys," he croaked. "What's going on?"

"Kevin! You're alive!" shrieked Ms. Prince who had undone her fusion as Ajkar. Kevin managed a weak smile. Sadie, Jakey and Darren grasped him in a huge bear hug. Kevin gasped in pain and they released, solemnly apologizing to him.

"So, what happened?" Kevin asked. They filled him in and he laughed after hearing Darren's note.

"You actually said that?" he asked in disbelief.

"Wrote it actually, with Sadie's help of course." He replied.

"Well then, let's go away from here, and have ourselves a good well earned lunch."

Ms. Prince shook her head. "No, you actually can't until the tournament is won. You see, we are given the power by God to do this. No one can undo it until its purpose has been fulfilled. You guys have to finish the tournament."

Kevin stared in disbelief. "What? You aren't going to send us to fight again with that thing, are you?"

Ms. Prince sighed. "I have to. God made it so that in order for it to finish, there had to be one team standing. So, you guys have to keep going and beat all of the other teams in order to go back."

"What? Can't you ask him to make an exception?" Kevin asked.

Ms. Prince shook her head solemnly. " No, I can't."

Kevin walked away, his team following and then he turned around and said,

"Well, Ms. Prince, we'll make sure that we beat the teams qui-" he was cut short by a huge burst of leaves in front of him. Kevin flew into the air and landed a few feet away. Debris and trees were scattered around everywhere and there in front of him was a twenty-foot long abyss of black. Next to him was the tall, looming figure of Spargatus. He charged Kevin and threw him across the clearing. Kevin was ready and braced himself for it, so when he hit the tree Spargatus threw him at, he only hurt himself. Limping up, Kevin drew his sword and charged at him. Spargatus flicked his tail and slammed it into Kevin's gut. He flew backwards and crashed into a pile of sticks. Spargatus slithered hungrily towards Kevin, losing his awareness of the others. Darren charged into him and blindsided him, throwing him to the ground. Darren withdrew his blade from its sheath and brought it down, only for it to be thrown away by Spargatus. He barreled Spargatus over and then they locked themselves in by gripping each other's arms. Darren was on top of Spargatus, head butting and kicking, and then Sadie stepped in and reopened his tail wound with her blade. Spargatus roared in pain and flipped Darren over his head and into the abyss, Darren's grip on him firm and tight. They plummeted into the abyss, swallowed by darkness, the boy and the serpent…

14
The Scepter Of David

"DARREN!" SCREAMED KEVIN as he rushed towards the abyss. He looked down into the pit and there was blackness and nothingness. He tried to control himself. This was not the first person that had died for him.

"No." he whispered into the chasm of darkness. He looked to the sky and screamed, " No!"

Before he burst, he buried his head into his open palms. Sadie crept up to him and whispered, " It's okay, Kevin."

"No, it's not," he growled. " He's gone and it's my fault. I should have helped him but I was too busy nursing my stupid wounds. I should have helped him. I should have…" he looked at the bottomless void, eyes dilated and averted to something else. Sadie turned her head to look at him, her eyes bloodshot and her face worn with tears. She was breathing heavily, and her hand was firmly held on her injured leg. She looked too, and gasped heavily, her eyes widening as much as Kevin's. There, on the far side of the treacherous chasm was a small form, a band of glittering gold on the back, and further into the pit was the utterly recognizable and unmistakable figure of Spargatus.

"Darren!" Kevin screamed, lunging from his stoop on the ground and one hundred percent sprinting vigorously towards Darren. Darren was making his way up the side of the pit, the dirt digging into his nails, the rocks biting his palms, his arms and legs screaming in protest, but he didn't give up. His breath had run out, and now he was panting for a breath of fresh air. He didn't care whether a forty foot long snake monster was coming for him, he only knew he had to give the precious thing across his back to Kevin. His mind had continually repeated the same line through his head, the same line that was pushing him on that very moment. *Left foot up, right hand up, right foot up, left foot up*, that same procedure resounding through his head. Then he saw Kevin running for him, his pace never slowing, nothing hindering him. He was gradually making his way towards Darren, his pace quickening with every step. Then trouble came. Darren was getting closer and closer to the top, so close that he could actually see it. Then he felt a tug, a resistance pulling him back. He looked down to see his foot snagged on a deep indent in the rock. He tugged, but it only made it worse. Pain flared through his leg. While he struggled, Kevin progressed. Kevin was mere feet away from Darren now. He made it to where Darren was fighting to make it up. Darren twisted his leg, but the pain shot through his body. He looked down at his foe. Spargatus was gaining on him. He quickly shouldered the gold stick from his back with four silver horns and held in them was a large opal, shining bright. His instincts told him he had seconds.

"Kevin!"

Kevin's head poked out from the opening, his green eyes concerned.

"Darren, come on! Quick! He's gaining!" Darren turned to see Spargatus inches from his foot. He felt his foot crushed under the immense weight of Spargatus.

"Kevin! Here take this!" he threw the stick from his hand. Kevin deftly caught it with one hand, his other outstretched towards Darren.

"Come on! I've got you!"

Darren sighed and a tear streaked down his face.

"No," he said, Spargatus's hand clenching his head. "You don't." he let go, a look of shock and sadness along with pain crossing his face. But he hadn't gone down alone. Spargatus went, tumbling after him.

"No!" Kevin screamed. He dropped the stick and stepped back. He readied himself to run. He threw himself forward.

"Kevin!" Jakey threw himself into Kevin, barreling him over.

"Jakey! What- what was that for?"

Jakey was out of breath. "I- pant was saving- pant you from killing yourself! We don't know how deep that thing is! It could be hundreds of feet deep."

Kevin then realized what he had been about to do. He also realized it couldn't be that deep if Darren had ran in, grabbed something, and climbed most of the way up in close to thirty minutes.

"I am so sorry for scaring you like that and making you have to save me. Would you like a cookie?"

Jakey glowered evilly at him.

"Shut up."

Kevin looked into the hole of death. Tears began to flow freely from his eyes, never ending waterfalls.

"I could have- no! Should have saved him! It's not fair! It's not fair!" he looked up to the sky and screamed.

"What did I ever do to you Lord? I did nothing!" he screamed the last words out, and then hit the ground.

Ms. Prince, followed by everyone else came to Kevin. She and Sadie too were crying. So was Jakey.

"Why? Why?" Kevin wailed.

 Kevin," Ms. Prince said wiping tears from her face. " We all have to move on in life. And you do know you have t-"

"NO! I WILL NOT ACCEPT IT!" Kevin roared.

Ms. Prince turned to the others.

"We'll leave him here. You two, get a fire going."

"What are you going to do?" Jakey inquired.

"I'm going to find out what it is Darren lost his life for."

Hours. They passed by like birds in the sky. By the time that Ms. Prince had found her information, books had piled around her, and everyone was asleep. Next to the fire, curled in his own jacket, Jakey lay, his fair hair shining gold in the firelight. Sadie was lightly snoozing, her blades drawn and still clenched tightly in her hands. She looked to the pit's edge. A huddled figure, deep tan skin and black curly hair, a mess and strewn across the head huddled, momentarily drifting into reality and saying "No." and then slipping into slumber. She looked at Kevin. He was the exact opposite of a hero, yet he deserved the scepter. He was the rightful heir, but she held back. He was small, no bigger than Benji. His hair corkscrewed around his head with one slightly falling messily onto his forehead. He was muscular in his own aspect. Strength and power rippled under him yet he was scrawny. His beige skin was scarred in multiple places on his bare arms and his neck bore a scar where two claws had intersected while cutting him, making an L that was only visible if he looked up. He was clad in casual attire, his white sweater no longer white, but a dirty brown and his cargoes ripped, torn and wet with what seemed to be blood. She scowled. She didn't want to give it to him but it was necessary. She roused each of them from their slumber. Jakey stood upright and asked, " Did you find anything out?" She nodded unhappily and glared at Kevin.

"He better know how to use it though." She grumbled unhappily.

"Know how to use wha-" The stare Aurorua and Ms. Prince gave him was enough to shut him up. She woke up Sadie and moved to Kevin. She pressed her hand gently to his back.

"Kevin, it's time to get up." He turned over to her, his scar a gruesome and bloody sight, red-crimson pasted across his neck and head.

"No." he said defiantly, his deep sapphire eyes glaring into her. She said nothing and walked to the other two.

"Sit down." They sat down obediently and were quiet, waiting for an answer.

"Well, it all began in the time of King David of Jerusalem. He ordered his-"

"Wait, we're not supposed to be listening to a story, though. We're supposed to be learning about that," Jakey said, pointing to the scepter.

"Shut up. She knows what she's doing." growled Sadie. Jakey was silent.

"Thank you Sadie, I couldn't have said it better."

"So, in the time of King David it began. One day, David had ordered his priests to make a scepter. It would be two feet long, with silver ram's horns and an opal in the middle of it. Decorated in gold, the horns were to come from a regular rams horn and they were to be encased in silver. Later on, John the Disciple found it and filled it with blood. On the inside of them was the blood, the Blood of Jesus. The blood was supposed to resurrect anyone or thing from the dead. Called the Scepter of David, it had been guarded as an ancient artifact until Jesus died. Then the Devil mounted an attack on the defenders of the Scepter, and it was taken right into the hands of Spargatus, the Serpent. Now it is back in our hands, yet the only wielder is a descendant of David."

"So," Sadie began, "The only wielder for The Scepter of David is…"

They all took a long look at the huddled figure near the pit.

"There's our wielder," said Ms. Prince angrily.

15
The Hunt

"*THE HEIR TO* the scepter of David is you Kevin, you must take it."

Kevin walked over, picked it up and dropped his sword. He shuffled away into the darkness, Pfen in tow.

Kevin, we should wait. Pfen warned.

No. I have to do this. Plus, I want to try something on the big snake. Kevin growled, then rejected an oncoming tear. He trudged on, and continued, feeling the ground every few moments with his hand and moving on.

So, what's the plan?

Well, we go into the pit, and then we track down the snake.

His name is Spargatus, as if you care. What next?

We kill him and- Pow! We rescue Darren. Kevin smiled smugly with his plan.

You're an idiot. Pfen said.

"Then what do I do, smarty?"

Wait. We need help then- a loud noise pierced the night sky.

What was that?

Dunno; let's keep moving though

Gotcha. They continued on, scouring the pit for an opening. When they made their way back to the fire, Kevin told Pfen,

There's only one way in. He nodded towards the chasm.

No! That's not going to help unless you want to get us both killed!

Kevin grinned devilishly. *We can do this.*

Stupid fool.

Kevin slipped in, thinking he was unnoticed and crept towards his old sword. He strapped it over his shoulder and crept away. Were it not for the pans next to his foot, he would have crept away unnoticed. He slammed his toe into one and yelped in pain. He swung towards the other direction to see if he had roused anyone and his hand connected with yet another pan. *Clang!*

"Ow!" he screeched and swore silently.

"Who's there?" Ms. Prince stood up and stared at Kevin.

"What're you doing?" she inquired.

Kevin growled and said angrily, "Saving my friend." He then turned and this time, Jakey wasn't there to stop him. At full run, Kevin threw himself into the pit, Pfen right behind him…

Falling took forever. Kevin felt like he had been falling for hours. He kept glancing down, and then he began to realize just how stupid he was. He felt as if he were moving to the side, as if not going down, but left and right. He looked to his right, yet the wall seemed to be far away. Then he looked to his left. The wall, tall, and seemingly never-ending was closer than his thumb was to his hand, which was pretty close.

"AAAAHHHHH!!!!" he screamed, yet his voice was lost in the whistling of the wind. He stared at the bundle hovering over him.

"Pfen!" he screamed, yet his voice was lost in the screaming wind. Then impact came, and when it did, Kevin was unprepared. His body, small and delicate, ricocheted off of the left wall. A foreign pain arced through his left arm, reopening his old fang bite. Kevin winced.

"You will die." He spoke to no one in particular, yet his words had a meaning in them. After that, Spargatus had shuddered as if he had heard the words. Kevin didn't brace himself to hit the bottom. He simply tucked himself into a dive, Pfen screaming for mercy behind him. When impact came, it was hard.

"Kevin!" Ms. Prince screamed, which awakened both Sadie and Jakey who bumped heads and then punched each other on the shoulders until they were satisfied.

"I lost him." She said.

"What?" Sadie asked. Jakey playfully punched her on the arm. She slammed her fist into his face, and he flew backwards. Her face was completely focused. Jakey came up, rubbing a sore nose and a bruised eye.

"Dude, what was that for? I mean-" he never finished. Sadie first uppercut him and then round housed him and knocked him senseless with a stick of fire wood and then put the wood back where it had been.

"Continue." she said.

Darren had survived the fall again, yet this time he wasn't sure he would live. His leaf blade was bent in an odd position, as if a metal human had sat on it until it bent to its will. He threw it down and inspected his wounds. Blood flowed freely from a large gash on the side of his head, and his flank looked as if a spear had impaled it. His legs had failed him due to exhaustion and deprivation of blood, and he had fallen down in a crevasse, hoping the serpent wouldn't find him. Apart from scratches, bruises and cuts, his arms were fine. One of his legs was soaked in so much blood he didn't know what it was that was making him bleed there. The other had gone numb, and he believed he had broken it beyond repair. He squinted into the darkness, blood and sweat clouding his vision as he looked. He heard a shuffle in the darkness. Spargatus had arrived…

Kevin looked up. His injuries were minimal, but the thing that annoyed him was that his bite had reopened. He didn't care, and stood up. He had work to do and he wouldn't be accomplishing anything by sitting there. Pfen licked his forehead and he patted him on the head. He stood up and began to follow a long trail, with footprints and smudge marks. He had started. The hunt had begun.

16
Found

DARREN FELT SHARP claws boring into his skin. They dug deeper and deeper, every moment Darren screaming silently. Spargatus had found him, and he was prey to the predator. He slowly and cautiously picked up his leaf blade and swung it over his shoulder. *Boink!* There was a muffled hiss and then Darren shot out of his hiding place, crawling on the ground. Spargatus shook his head and snarled at him. Charging recklessly, Spargatus couldn't be stopped. Darren's defeat was inevitable.

Kevin hauled himself over a large boulder, his left leg aching and screaming in protest. Pfen had turned into a bloodhound and was slowly moving closer and closer towards Darren. Kevin's heart had skipped a beat. *I can make things right for once.* Then he remembered the people who had died for him, and he had done nothing. Pfenolus, the boy with the gorilla, and, his Mom and Dad, they had died and he had done nothing. Nothing. He would avenge them. That he knew, and there was only one way to do it. Kill Spargatus. Pfen howled and flew through the tunnels.

"Wait up!" Kevin yelled, but Pfen was off. He charged after, holding the scepter up. It began to glow, turning fiery red and destroying the bluish tinge of the place. He gaped and then refocused his attention. It was silent for a moment, and all Kevin could hear was water drip, drip, dripping. He perked up, and his heart began to race. He heard a loud hiss, and another, louder this time. And another, yet another. Kevin, being a sensible human, he did the sensible thing. He ran. He was now running for his life, Pfen dragged along and now, he was not hunting, but being hunted.

Sadie swore that if she ever got her hands on Kevin, he would wish he had never been born. Yet she knew where that ferocity in him had come from. He wanted to prove that he was useful. That nobody had to die for him anymore, that he was important. She understood that, yet she was angry. No matter how much she wanted to slap him, she knew why he was doing this. She strapped her swords on and Jakey did the same, rubbing a large welt on his head.

"You know," he said, " Your fists hurt."

Sadie turned to see him and laughed.

"What? Sadie. Tell- me-what-you-did." he said sternly.

"I busted up your face."

"Oh." he said, and then said, noticing what she just said,

"Oh no you didn't." he ran at her and she sidestepped, tripping him and picking him up by the scruff.

"You forget that Kevin and Darren are gone and that my patience runs out quickly. Now get up, and get ready to save Kevin and Darren."

"Gotcha. Please don't kill me." He whined. She shoved him to the ground and said, "Let's go. And I don't want to see you get up if you're going to get in trouble."

Jakey didn't move.

"Why aren't you going?" Sadie asked.

"You told me not to go if I was going to get in trouble."

"So you're going to get in trouble?"

Jakey pretended to be writing on an imaginary checklist with his hand.

"Yup. Says it here." He said, showing her his open, and empty palm. She slammed her fist into his face and he flew backwards.

"Oww! What was that for?" Jakey whined, rubbing his bruised cheek.

"Let's go." Sadie said. Ms. Prince was right behind them, Aurorua behind her, and Benji beside Sadie along with Howlin on Jakey's shoulder.

"Grant!" Ms. Prince shouted into the dark forest. Grant stepped forward, materializing from behind a tree. Jakey flinched and then resumed his posture.

"Yes?" he asked, Thundarx grunting next to him.

"Get the other team out, cut their circlets and tell them the tournament is canceled. This has gone too far. I could have dealt with this if it hadn't gone this far, but two children are dead, another two ready to die, and so help me God, I shall not allow any more to die. And that Ruach. That Ruach is interfering with the forest transformation technique."

He did a short bow and ran away, with quick, and breathless bursts.

"Wait, wait, wait, you're not going without us." Sadie said, Benji grunting approvingly next to her.

"There never was a way of turning your mind. Stubborn girl."

"Me too." Jakey piped.

Ms. Prince nodded and then they all threw themselves at the tunnel, swallowed by the darkness of night and the pit.

"Pfen?" Kevin called to his companion.

Kevin? You there? Pfen asked.

Yeah, and we've got company. Pfen looked up and saw Spargatus just in time to see the death barb rocketing towards his head. He ducked and Kevin fought; yet his blade felt dull and heavy. He sliced up and hit home. Spargatus screeched in pain and clutched his chest. He slammed his tail into Kevin's chest and he flew back, hitting a sheer rock wall. He slumped over.

"Pfen, Let's do it." Kevin croaked. Pfen walked towards him, time slowing. Kevin could see streaks of light flying by his face. Gray, black, red, blue green, and more. Then he got up. He was no longer Kevin and Pfen was no longer Pfen. They were one. They were the Duo. They were, Kevin thought. What would they call themselves? He didn't know or care. Spargatus stepped back, in fear and doubt of fighting such a powerful force. The being in front of him was great. With the stature of a man, and the tail, claws, legs body and head of a wolf, Kevin and Pfen created a powerful being, masculine and terrifying. The eyes glittered, a deep sapphire, yet one was blue and the other was Pfen's silver eye color. Across their back was a bow, and strapped to a long belt was the Scepter. On their back, large black and silver dappled wings shone pure and deadly. Kevin decided they would call themselves Pfenoli.

Pfenoli stepped together as one and they did something new to Kevin. In their hand, they withdrew the Scepter. Pfenoli punched it into the ground and it began to crack and splinter. A bright light began to shine and snake towards Spargatus. He was backing away in fear now, retreating far away from Pfenoli. Pfenoli put his palm to the opal and then the Scepter turned into a full-length sword, a bronze hilt with the silver horns sprouting as a hand guard, sleek and deadly. The blade itself was beautiful. It was deep obsidian, yet silver and gold at the same time. It was all of them. Pfenoli's blade whistled as it sliced like a knife through butter in Spargatus' skin. Spargatus was hissing and spitting and retreating and roaring in agony. He was no longer classified as winning.

Pfenoli made an uppercut motion with his blades and sent Spargatus packing. He slithered into the darkness, and Kevin heard no more. They unformed, Kevin feeling a short *whoosh* of wind go through his body and then they were separate.

"So," Kevin said, " what do we do now?"

Darren lay there, hearing the battle going on feet away. Spargatus had slithered by angrily not two minutes ago, rubbing wounds and wincing.

Kevin? He thought.

"Kevin?" he croaked meekly.

"Darren?" Kevin shouted into the darkness. "You there?"

"Kevin. Over here." Kevin crept forward, Pfen glancing around, leaping at everything that he passed. Kevin looked at Darren.

"Darren, is that you?"

"Yes it's me!" he snarled.

Kevin scooped him up and propped him up, with Darren leaning on his shoulder. He began to make his way in the opposite direction, towards the opening. Darren slowed him down in his armor, yet it was still okay, they were making their way along steadily and slowly towards it. Once in the center, Kevin looked up at the light, it's dull shine giving him sight.

He looked around, scanning for a way out. Then, he saw a large rocky slope that spiraled up and ended close to the top. He and Darren began to lope towards their exit. Then they heard a noise. It rumbled in the tunnels, and then shook the rocks. Then, dark shapes flooded the room, blades glinting, spears in the air and bat shaped wings fluttering in the air too. *Wings?* Kevin drew his sword and looked around at the hundreds of Brechen surrounding him and Darren.

"Stay back!" Kevin shouted nervously, turning his Scepter into a blade with a quick palm swipe, holding the blade out. The Brechen around him screeched in terror at the sight of it.

"Get- away- from- me!" Kevin screamed through gritted teeth. Then, he lost it as a shape loomed out in front of him. Not Spargatus yet one from a deeper past. It was here. The thing that killed him. That killed Pfenolus. Kevin glared with hatred. He despised its kind, and apparently, it despised him too. Kevin swiped his palm over the opal and he now held his Scepter. He brought it up, and drove it into the ground. A force, invisible, yet deadly, threw him back, into Pfen who was guarding the injured Darren. A huge shock of fire and electricity flew at the Brechen. Knocking them over like pins it continued, the closest ones being snapped and broken on impact. Kevin stood up, wincing and rushed over to retrieve his Scepter. A foot, human, planted itself in the ground on Kevin's outstretched right arm.

"You should be dead. And," he said, plucking the Scepter with his hand, "this is mine."

Kevin gasped in pain and looked up, his mouth falling open. The hooked nose, blonde hair, sharp features, muscular frame, they led to one person, the man who tried to kill him.

"Tie them up. Spargatus will want to see this." His eyes were dismissive as Brechen began to crawl over their dead comrade's bodies. Darren put up no struggle. He was unconscious by the time they got there. Pfen growled and leaped at the first Brechen, teeth bared. He bit him on the neck, his teeth sinking deep.

"Get it off me! I'll rip out it's hide, I'll-" He didn't finish. Pfen drew himself from his fallen foe, his teeth shining with silver blue blood. The Brechen soon turned to a puddle, reduced to nothing. In all, it took four Brechen to restrain Pfen, six less than Kevin. They had held him from all sides, the man injecting him and Pfen going limp. Kevin screamed into the gag that held his mouth shut. His foe turned, smiling evilly at him.

"So, Listener, you up to be target practice?"

Sadie, Jakey and Ms. Prince had landed, Sadie who felt like her arm had broken, and Jakey being winded by the impact of the ground, his stomach lurching, and tempting to hurl. It did. He ran over to the wall, and wretched all over it. It felt like more, but the jump was at the most twenty feet. He rolled over, gasping for breath. A hand materialized next to him.

"Need help?" Sadie asked, her arm already lifting him up. Benji was right next to her as always, quiet and solitary. Howlin would be on his way.

"Yeah, thanks." Jakey said, dusting himself off. He looked at her pale shoulder.

"What happened?" he asked.

"Broke it." Sadie said jokingly.

"I'm just kidding. Just hurt it really bad."

Ms. Prince walked up, and said, strapping her twin blades across her back,

"Let's move." She walked off, Sadie and Jakey scrambling to see her through the darkness.

"Howlin?" Jakey asked.

"Yes, Jakey?" Howlin's voice was old and croaky, something close to and old man's, yet there was something behind it. Howlin's head turned to one side, and rocks, small crumbles and shavings, flew off in different directions.

"Can you see?"

"No, but I hear something." Each companion's ears perked up, ready and alert. Aurorua growled, eager and ready for battle. Howlin stretched his wings and hooted defensively. Benji stared up, teeth bared, and muscles tense. A battle raged on in front of them. They felt a loud blast of air, then it knocked them flat and bashed them to the ground. Sadie screamed in pain, as her broken arm collided with the rock wall. Jakey gasped, his stomach lurching while a rock slammed into his gut. Ms. Prince stayed up, slicing rocks that flew her way in half. Howlin slammed into a wall and closed his eyes momentarily, yet they opened back up and he dived at Jakey, knocking into him and pecking. Jakey got up.

"What?"

"Kevin. He-" Howlin's sentence was interrupted by a loud scream that was stifled by something. Jakey charged into the opening, looking at the tunnels. He saw scuffle marks and followed them to the chamber that Kevin and Darren had been dragged through. He saw a hole, out in the open. He poked his head in, hearing a loud clamor and commotion. He gasped. There was Kevin, bound and gagged; his head hung low and his face bloody. He was being dragged deeper in, and was now far from Jakey. Jakey lunged forward, but it was too late. A rock rolled in front of him, blocking his path to Kevin...

17
Captured

"KEVIN!" JAKEY WAILED. Howlin began to slam his beak into the rock, relentlessly. He chipped his beak and fluttered to the ground. Jakey slammed his fists into the rock, every time his hand staining more and more crimson. He heard thuds as Sadie, Benji, Ms. Prince and Aurorua approached.

"I lost him." Jakey said, head hung low.

"It's okay." Sadie said, her voice quivering with each word.

"No, it's not. I should have helped him. And I- I saw him too. He was tied up and gagged."

"What did he look like?"

"Bloody. There was blood everywhere. His eyes were drooped, and some huge thing was dragging him on the ground."

"What did it look like?" Ms. Prince asked.

"It was green, with bumps, and there were teeth sticking from the arms and it looked like a lizard. And, it stood up on two legs, and-" he faltered. "It had swords instead of arms."

"Ephanashim." Ms. Prince said quietly.

"Epha what?" Jakey asked, confusion twisting his features.

"Ephanashim. The snake-man. Cursed by God, and turned to that. A mouthful of sharp teeth with a bad attitude." Ms. Prince said, shaking her head.

"Well, that ephonasham or whatever it's called was taking Kevin somewhere. To that snake thing, I think."

"Yeah, and we have to help him."

They heard a noise, then pebbles and rocks hitting the ground. Jakey looked up at the stone.

"What the-"

"Run! Quickly!" Ms. Prince hissed quietly.

They obeyed, and ran off, Jakey in the lead. Once they were around a corner, they turned and looked. Led by the Ephanashim, was a small troop of Brechen, armed with short dirks and bows, with quivers of crude "Search the place. Master wants it searched and wants those mortals found." the Ephanashim said, his voice deep and gruff.

"Yes sir." said a Brechen.

"Good. Sunt, take two to that tunnel," He said, indicating the right tunnel in a fork.

"Purch, you and the other two go to the left, and I'll take the middle."

"Yes sir," said one with a hooked horn that had a golden band on the end, decorated in intricate gems, and carved with images and symbols.

Jakey looked over the ridge, where they had taken the left path.

"I need that bracelet," he said lustily, his fingers closing on his knife.

"What did you say?" Sadie asked him.

"Nothing." he whispered.

"We'll take them when they're deep in and then make a run for the tunnel," Ms. Prince said, pointing to the large, and brightly lit tunnel that was behind where the rock had been. The Brechen came, bickering over how they would eat the three humans.

"We should boil them in a stew."

"No," another said, "We should roast them over a spit."

"Stew."

"Roast."

"Stew!"

"Roast!"

"Shut up!" hissed Purch. "Or else Epharlan will cook and roast the both of you!" snarled Purch. They were silent, and tramped through the tunnel, unaware of the waiting humans. Suddenly, a knife, deep black and shining was sticking through the Brechen in the back of its neck, and then another was buried in the forehead of the second, while three blades stuck themselves into Purch's heart, chest and head. Each Brechen fell, knocked over like bowling pins by an invisible bowling ball. Sadie, Jakey, Ms. Prince and their companions stepped into the tunnel, striding forward toward the fallen Brechen. Jakey withdrew his knife from Purch's heart and cleaned it on his skin while sliding the bracelet onto his wrist. He marveled at it, sheathing his blade. He heard a soft *shink* as the three Brechen dissolved into puddles.

"Aren't you a beauty?" he said to the bracelet.

"Come on, Jakey, stop looking at your spoils of battle." Sadie said. They moved back to their tunnel position in a small hollow on the right side of the tunnel, and waited.

Kevin's eyes blinked open as he batted them back and forth to break the blood that sealed them closed. He groaned momentarily and looked around. He saw a fire under a stone that hung from the wall and then he saw- Wait! He was upside down, hanging from the ceiling, which was why everything was upside down. His head began to throb, and then he heard a thud next to his ear. He turned and saw a knife sticking out of the wall not an inch from his cheek. He looked forward and saw a group of Brechen led by that man holding, aiming and throwing long and thin knives at him. He panicked and yelped, which sent a volley of knives at him. One sunk into his right thigh, forcing him to yelp in pain, yet he couldn't finish when three flew into his arm and another sank into his ear. He screamed in agony and attempted to nurse his ear with his shoulder, since his hands were bound. The Brechen prepared again, squinting, leaning back and throwing. One flew into his foot, another two clipping his forehead and falling off, and one more slicing his chest. The fifth went too high and sliced the rope in half, dropping the limp Kevin to the ground.

"Idiot! How could you miss?" growled the man.

"S-sorry sir, sorry s-s-" he didn't finish, for a throwing knife had buried itself into his heart. The unlucky beast melted into a puddle.

"Oops, must have slipped," the man said, glaring at the other three, none of them saying anything against him.

"Go tie him back up. I've lost my taste for target practice," he said angrily. Once they had tied Kevin back up, the man stalked off, disappearing into the darkness. Kevin looked up as they tied him back up. He groaned, and was silenced by a fist. He felt the blades slicing through his skin as they were removed, making him moan in pain. They walked away, Kevin's vision going fuzzy, then black.

The Ephanashim, Epharlan, grunted as he made his way back, empty-handed. He had scouted the area, using his power to try to sense them, yet he couldn't. He returned to the chamber, the group that went to the left not returning, while the group that went to the right came back, empty-handed as he. He grunted quietly at the left tunnel, motioning them towards it. They moved on, Epharlan taking the back of the group. The lead one, Surc, gasped as they neared the massacre of the other three Brechen.

"Wetness. They must have Purdled." Surch whispered to the others. The weapons still lay on the ground. Surch scoured the piles with his slits,

"If you see a golden bracelet, it's mine." He growled towards the others.

"No." a voice behind him growled. He looked back into glaring red eyes belonging to Epharlan. One of his arms came up and down. "It's mine." A new puddle had been added to the other three. Then, blades sang. One flew into one of the Brechen's heads, while another flew through the neck. They didn't know what hit them. Epharlan felt his eye become excruciatingly painful and looked with the other, scouring the area for the thrower. Another blade sank into his thigh and another flew into his belly button. He roared in pain, the blade that stuck into his belly button popping out.

"Who are you?" he growled to the assailants. "Show yourselves!"

"Are you sure?" a voice called.

"Get out now, and I will ease your passing." A black, sleek shape darted out, the shape of Ajkar.

"Get ready to die." He hissed.

"You sure you want to do this?" the feminine voice called to him.

"Yes," he snarled, throwing the two black knives, one that went into his eye, and the other that went into his thigh. Ajkar deftly caught them by the handle, preparing a battle stance.

"Let's dance."

"Kevin. Kevin." The voice of Darren was irreplaceable. It was soft and silky, yet worn like leather. As if he were a child, yet there was something different behind those hazel eyes, something knowing and understanding. Kevin turned. His armor was gone; the only thing he wore was a rag across his waist that the Brechen had pinned grotesquely with knives, which had bloodied his legs.

"You all right?" he asked.

"Yeah, but I think my legs'll fall off before I die." Darren said.

"Don't say that. We'll get out. Somehow. We just have to have hope in-"

"God?" the voice of that man made Kevin shudder. "You want to put your faith in a god who doesn't even care?"

"He cares." Kevin said.

"If he did, wouldn't he save you from these ' bad men'?" he said sarcastically.

"He's faithful. He'll help." Kevin said defiantly.

"You want to know something? Take the apostrophe out of he'll and then you'll know where I am taking you." He turned around, laughed and strode away. Kevin and Darren mouthed the word together and exchanged nervous looks.

"We have to get out of here." Kevin said.

"You think?" Then they heard something, a soft yipping. Kevin turned his head to see familiar silver eyes looking up at him.

18
Rescue

AJKAR SLIPPED THROUGH Epharlan's legs, slicing his right one, which brought him down on a knee. They whirled around and jumped onto his back, hanging on by the blades that had sunken into his back. He roared in pain and slammed Ajkar to the rocks, the stealthy feline woman gracefully leaping away, an arm outstretched and blade flashing. It carved a long path down the side of his head. He growled and arced his blade in a circular motion, swinging it towards the two children. White met green as Benji bulldozed into the great beast. They tumbled over, biting, kicking, slashing and ripping at each other. When they came out, Epharlan was on top, suffering from a handful of injuries. Bite and scratch marks peppered his bare arms, oozing blue blood. His stomach was ripped open by a large claw wound and his face was painted cobalt. He brought his sword up on Benji, who was bleeding on his side and his forehead. Then, a loud chink! was heard as a rock collided with his head. The large creature slumped over, nearly crushing Benji, who was able to scamper away. Jakey giggled, and then raised his hand.

"I did that."

"I'm sure you did," Sadie said. Jakey grinned. "But, it didn't dissolve. Why is that Ajkar?" she asked.

"He is not dead."

"What?" Jakey whined. "That would have killed any human, so why didn't it kill him?"

"An Ephanashim is not human." Ms. Prince said, running a hand through her hair, which was tousled, from a blast of air that had come when she and Aurorua had separated.

"Oh really, I wouldn't have noticed that." Jakey said sarcastically.

"We have to go, now." She whispered hurriedly.

"What do we do?"

"Save Kevin and Darren." She said, pointing to the large boulder that was rolling into place, cutting off their path. Jakey whined,

"Why can't this ever be easy?!"

"Pfen! I missed you!" Kevin exclaimed as he saw his companion again.

Missed you too. Pfen spoke quickly and hurriedly, his shape already changing to that of Benji. He growled, bent his knees and pounced, claws outstretched as he sliced through the ropes. Kevin and Darren dropped to the ground. Pfen's form began to change, his skin turning rough, and hard and gray. Tusks began to sprout from his mouth, white and hard as rock. His ears grew, losing their fur, and turning gray and bumpy. His hide thickened and grew, and finally in place of a wolf, there was a large bull elephant. Kevin and Darren couldn't climb on, so Pfen slipped his trunk under them, and lifted them up. They slid down and onto his back. Before they began their escape, he snatched up two bows with quivers of arrows. As he slowly lumbered on, Kevin and Darren's bows were trained and alert, as they watched for a Brechen to come out. Darren had tried asking, "Hawksbeak, Hawksbeak." But Kevin had said that they would have to get him after, when they had recovered. Pfen's trunk trumpeted, a long wail echoing in the dark, and he charged forward, trampling Brechen as they attempted to stop him, while Kevin and Darren had shot their arrows, doing it carefully, and knowing that they would have to hit their mark every time. Darren was fatigued though and had to lie down. His head resting in the small crevasse of where the neck and body met, he curled up, into a ball and fell asleep. Kevin heard a roar and turned to see Epharlan charging forward, his swords already raised. He yelled and then turned to the front. A couple hundred yards away, the way out shone, although something else shone, bright and gold. It was to his right, another forty or so yards to the left of the exit. Kevin whispered to Pfen and then hopped off, slinging both quivers over his back. Pfen turned around and confronted the army of Brechen, his trunk flared out, careful not to drop the unsuspecting Darren. Kevin was limping closer to Hawksbeak, his breath becoming ragged and heavy as he went. He was now a hundred yards away, every moment or so looking back to see the fight. He made his way to the armor, his fingers closing around it, and then he felt it, not the leathery skin, but something else. He grabbed where the sword should have been, but his hand closed on emptiness. He panicked and turned around. Something he didn't expect met him. Spargatus, the huge snake was nearing him…

Jakey's hand scraped a rock for the third time, this time blood spilling from his knuckles. He gritted his teeth and continued on, drawing his blade as they all had done, tramping through a sewer-like environment. He heard a commotion at the end of the hall, and pursued it. They all sped up behind him. As they made their way there, the clashing of swords grew louder, and something else. Trumpeting.

"Kevin." Jakey muttered. Ms. Prince stepped forward, already turning into Ajkar.

"Let's go." they said. While Sadie and Benji stepped forward, Jakey found himself stepping back.

"I-I'm not so sure about this."

"Do you want to save Kevin or not?"

Jakey sighed and followed them, every noise making him whimper silently.

"Ajkar," Sadie said, "Not good."

As they looked down, they saw Pfen, bleeding from multiple sword injuries. Around him lay the broken bodies of hundreds of Brechen, already dissipating into puddles of cobalt. Jakey heard a yell and turned to see a bloody Kevin, above him the serpent, Spargatus.

"No, no, no," He said, already running forward, Sadie behind him, with Ajkar further behind. As they neared, Spargatus' teeth closed around Kevin's mid section, his scream echoing through the chambers. Spargatus lifted his head; the limp Kevin folded inside of his grasp. Jakey rushed at the creature, jumping on and stabbing it. Spargatus screamed and dropped Kevin, and if it hadn't been for Pfen, he would have died. The elephant ran towards Kevin, catching him in mid-air. Kevin's flaccid body shook as his companion caught him. Jakey was steadily making his way up the snake until a loud roar was heard, coming from where Pfen had been fighting. Sadie, who was stabbing the monster turned and shouted to the others, "Run!"

The oncoming force, hundreds of Brechen led by Epharlan, marched towards them, spears extending from the front ranks. Pfen charged through them, diverting their attention as Sadie grabbed Darren's armor. Ajkar ran into the darkness, their stealthy body lurking through it as they searched for a room. As they made their way to an open cavern, a cold hand pressed to their mouth. A small knife slithered deathly close to their throat.

"Drop your sword, or I will kill you." Their swords clattered to the ground, then they heard the voice again.

"Now, you die anyways." The knife began to scratch Ajkar's neck, drawing blood but then Ajkar's elbow slammed into the man's groin, which made him keel over and gasp for air. Ajkar jumped into the air, spun, and their feet connected with his face about four times, already knocking him out by the first hit. He fell to the ground and stayed there. Ajkar entered the room, their blades sinking into the guard Brechen's neck. The Brechen fell prostrate on the ground, his body flapping weirdly. She made her way to the carcass of what used to be girl, merely a broken skeleton. Ajkar's hands closed around the Scepter. As they made their way to the exit, the man was getting up.

"Hey you-" Ajkar's foot connected with his face and he was knocked to the ground again. They slid past the commotion and made their way out. As they left, a short whoosh of air separated Ms. Prince and Aurorua. Their comrades were waiting for them, already running away. Ms. Prince turned and looked back. The brute Ephanashim was recklessly charging, along with Spargatus and the remaining Brechen. She cursed and continued on, Aurorua right next to her. In the distance, she heard a trumpet and assumed that the children were well on their way out. She ran, her heart beating and sandals pounding. She didn't dare look back and waste precious time. She remembered Kevin, loosely dangling in the jaws of the monster; his broken and limp form caked in blood. She wiped tears away and continued running, never looking back, always looking forward.

Pain. It was a second life to Kevin right now, and he was living it to the fullest. He wheezed and clawed for breath as Pfen made his way up the long spiral that made led to the exit. Kevin scrambled in his mind, wondering how long he had been in this gloomy darkness. He thought that he had been in here for a day or so, but the way everything had happened, so slowly yet abruptly, completely contradicted what he thought. But there was light. There were his friends. Sadie. Jakey. Darren. Pfen. He smiled though it hurt and patted the thick hide of his companion, yet it was more of a light graze than a pat. He closed his eyes as a blinding light pounded his eyes, giving him a drumming sensation that didn't feel good in his forehead. He opened his eyes and saw them. His friends. And the children of Companion Orphanage, and the teachers. Everyone, down to the cranky janitor with the cracked broom. He looked over at Sadie who was right next to him.

"Sadie," he said with a bit of effort. She turned her head.

"Kevin?" she said, trying hard not to show the effect all the blood had on her.

"We're back."

19
Hurt and Still Hurting

THREE WEEKS, AND he still felt sore. Kevin opened his eyes, but it hurt. He was in the orphanage hospital, a brightly lit room that smelled faintly of cinnamon. He looked around. As his eyes scanned, he found a dresser next to his reclining bed. On it was his flashlight and a charred piece of wood. *Hmm. They must have emptied my pockets.* He felt weight on the end of his bed. He saw the familiar dark blue pelt that covered a muscular shape. He smiled faintly. Pfen was a loyal companion. As Pfen slept, Kevin could see sparkles in his majestic pelt. It shone, true and beautiful. He moved his gaze to the rest of the room. A blue carpet was adorned with intricate decorations of companions, lions, wolves, tigers, and sharks; so many, that they spiraled to the center of the carpet. Kevin began to feel dizzy. His head hurt, and he pressed his fingers to it, hoping it would stop the pain. As he turned, he groaned in pain. His hand flew to his rib, and he found a bandage, blood still flowing under the bandage.

"Are you feeling better?" a voice said from the doorway. Kevin turned to the speaker. Sadie stood there, her right arm in a sling, the other on the side of her leg. She had propped herself up on the doorway. She wore a gray sweater, the hood hanging down. Her sweatpants were the same color, her blades strapped to each leg. Her black hair was tied back in a ponytail, and it shined as if she had just put something in it. Benji, tall and resolute, stood next to her.

"Can I come in?" she asked amiably.

"Yeah," Kevin managed weakly, the corners of his mouth stinging as he spoke. She walked in, smiling warmly at him.

"So, is Spargatus gone?" Kevin asked. Sadie nodded her head, and then shook it.

"What do you mean?" Kevin asked.

"Well, we got rid of the Brechen, but that Ephanashim, and Spargatus, well, they fled deeper in. Ms. Prince brought in some other Preservatives who should be able to track them down within a week."

"That's... good. I wonder, when am I getting out, did they tell you?" Sadie shook her head.

"Oh, okay." He sat up, wincing and holding his stomach as he did.

"It hurts?" Sadie asked. Kevin looked up at her, not even saying anything. She laughed, and said, "No, I meant how bad is it?" Kevin

"I think I'm gonna find out though." He lifted his shirt and peeled back one bandage. He gasped. A long, white gash slid across his ribcage, green veins evident, and strangely bent under it. They were bent, as if they had been severed in half. They still wriggled beneath his skin, giving Kevin a sickly feeling. He closed the bandage, and pulled down his shirt. The door opened, and Jakey stepped in, Howlin hopping closely behind.

"How're you doing?" Jakey asked.

"Horrible." Kevin said, smiling to his friend.

"So, I guess we have to wait for you, don't we?"

Kevin nodded his head.

"You know, when you got bit, and then we brought you here, I thought you were dead. You were all, like a zombie. It was creepy."

"Really?" Kevin asked Sadie. Jakey continued, clearing his throat to

"Yeah, you were all torn and bloody, and your arms were in the air, and you were muttering something about fire."

Fire? Man, Kevin must have been hurt!

"But then, Ms. Prince heard the Brechen howling and she went all karate on them!" Jakey recalled, making chopping motions with his hand while spinning around. He bumped into Sadie and stopped, looking sheepishly at his feet.

"Sorry."

She punched him on the arm. "It's okay." A woman, dressed in white wearing a nurse's coat walked in, carrying a tray of food. A steaming bowl of soup sat in the center, a juice box in the right hand corner. Under it was a spoon, and a straw. To the left of the soup, was a small package of crackers. Kevin tossed Jakey the crackers as the nurse checked his blood-rate and his temperature.

"You know," Jakey said, already pulling out a second cracker. "I could come back every day, and tell you what's going on."

Kevin shook his head and the nurse came back, holding a clipboard.

"Kevin, I'm Ms. Shard. I've been here giving you your food and making sure you have enough rest, and I think you can leave your bed, but you will be confined to crutches for a week, and you have to stay here, in the hospital." She suggested.

"Um, I'll go in the crutches." Kevin said. They brought in a pair at the end of the day, testing each one and twisting the screws to make it a perfect fit. Finally, they found him the right ones, and he asked them a question.

"Can I see a boy named Darren Hawkback?" The nurse nodded and motioned for him to follow her. They came to a broad desk in the center of the floor, and she typed a couple keys on the keyboard, and then she walked off, Kevin following her to a room marked 109. Under it was a small plastic screen with a slip in it, labeled DARREN H. He stepped in and saw his friend. A bandage covered his forehead, and crusted under its surface was tons of blood. His arm was in a sling, and his foot was raised, wrapped up like a mummy's. His friend's chest and stomach were inside of a white casing that kept him in one position. On seeing him, Darren smiled.

"So, I got pretty banged up, didn't I?"

Kevin nodded. "Yeah." He stepped forward, leaning on the crutches as he went, but he found it hard, since both legs were hurt. The nurse had said that the knives had damaged the ligaments, so he shouldn't put any weight on them.

"So, how are you?" Kevin asked.

"I've been worse. One time, when Hawksbeak and me were in the ocean, I forgot to dry myself. When I did, it was too late. Got pneumonia. Well, we were on a deserted island then, and *then*, only then was that bad. I nearly died, too, but then Hawksbeak left, and found me some friends. Ms. Prince. I'll never be able to repay her. She saved my life by believing in Hawksbeak when every other person ran for a gun to get his hide." He gazed wistfully out of the window at the sunset. "I'll never forget that. Never."

"So, what have you been doing?"

"Lessons."

"Lessons?" Kevin asked.

"Yeah, lessons. Ms. Prince isn't done with my 'improper grammar' yet." He said, smiling.

"Oh. Okay. So how do you feel?"

"Hurt and still hurting."

"I know the feeling. See you later, man."

Kevin walked off, making his way to his room. As he lay in his bed, he thought, *He's out there somewhere, and he won't stop until he has my blood...*

20
Shot In a Café

TWO FIGURES LOOMED over Kevin, red eyes glowering at him. He screamed, seeing the scarred face of Epharlan. The blades were hooked and cruel, menacing as they wandered over his head. He heard a hissing, and turned to the narrow, fine pointed features of Spargatus. He called for Pfen, but his companion was distant, and gone. Another figure, more human walked up. It was the man. Blonde hair covered his head, wispy and thin. He pulled out a gun, a pistol, aimed carelessly and shot Kevin.

"No!" He searched for the three figures, his eyes wild and his hair messy. The room though was dimly-lit and empty.

Pfen. Pfen. He called to his sleeping wolf. Pfen's head poked up, slowly and tiredly.

What? I only went to sleep a little while ago.

Yeah, whatever, but I think that they are still out there. Kevin emphasized the word they, so that Pfen knew what he meant.

Well, what do we do?

We- Kevin began, but Pfen cut him off.

We do nothing! Nothing! Nothing! Nothing! Okay? Nothing! N-O-T-H-I-N-G!!

Okay, then. Kevin rolled his eyes and nodded off to sleep.

"Kevin. You awake?" two eyes, red and peering precariously close to

Kevin's face greeted him as he awoke. He growled, and threw his head up, Jakey recoiling as Kevin did.

"Violence." Jakey tutted. "Bad choice. I guess I'll just go away…" Jakey trailed off, making his way to the door. Kevin's hand grabbed Jakey's leg, and tripped him, then grabbed a crutch and pressed it into Jakey's back.

"Ow! That hurts." Jakey said, rubbing his left knee as he got back up, Kevin's grip on Jakey with the crutch slackening.

"Sit down." Kevin said.

"No need to be pushy." He pulled over a chair, telling Kevin of the details of the day. By about three o'clock, Sadie walked in, Benji and Pfen running to greet each other as she walked over to Kevin.

"Hello Sadie." Kevin said.

"Hi Kevin."

"Wassup, my n-"

"Shut up." Jakey's hand came down and he pulled up his pants. He muttered something under his breath and then his face shot up, a goofy smile spread across it.

"So, you come here to stand around or to tell us something?" He asked.

Sadie ignored him and asked, "Want to go for a walk?"

Kevin's view of the world had been bleak for the years before CO. He hadn't been allowed outside, and he was home-schooled. He never left his house and when he asked, his mother would say, "You don't want to go there." As he stared at the towering skyscrapers, to the corner stores, Kevin couldn't help but stare in amazement. Why would his mother and Father not want him to see this? He had seen the world, but from the view of nature, with Storma and the wolf pack. Their orphanage was on a street called Dirk Street, which to Kevin made no sense since a dirk was a type of sword. As his feet scrambled across the rough-hewn pavement, Kevin couldn't help but wonder how great the world was. Pfen, who was small had been allowed to roam freely as they walked, since he looked like a dog. Howlin, however had taken to the sky, and Benji prowled around, the tiger moving so stealthily that you couldn't tell where he was at times. Kevin had brought some money, so they stopped at a hot dog stand in

Central Park, sitting on a bench to eat.

"This tastes good." Kevin said.

"You've never had a hot dog?" Jakey gazed in disbelief at Kevin. He shook his head.

"Humph. I'll bet you've never been outside." Kevin nodded and Jakey's hot dog dropped to the ground. Before he could do anything, Pfen was all over it, and when he was done, there was a piece of bread, smaller that Jakey's knuckle.

"Aww, man." He quickly forgot about it and then turned his attention to Kevin.

"So, my friend, you've never been to the big city?"

"Big city?" Kevin asked.

"'Big city'," Kevin shook his head. "'The city that never sleeps'?" Another head shake. "New York!" Jakey cried exasperatedly.

"New York?" Kevin asked.

"Oh my God." Jakey sighed. "You're a caveman. I have a friend who is a caveman. Great. Just gr-" a hot dog, ketchup, mustard, bun and all came whirling at him, splattering over his face and blue sweater.

"Ugh! What was that for?"

"Say what you said again and you'll get double treatment." snarled Kevin. Jakey wiped away a cluster of mustard that was hanging over his eye.

"Let me clean up." They made their way up the winding sidewalk, to a fast food restaurant. Jakey was in, and almost as quickly, he was out. His sweater was inside of his backpack, and he wore a red t-shirt. His jeans hadn't been splattered, and his shoes were dirty converses. His blonde hair was soaked wet from the water and his face was clean too.

"Let's go." As they left, the ground shook, knocking Kevin off of his feet. Tables and chairs flew across the room, knocking into the cashier. Chairs had become hurricanes, and rampaged around the shop, flying every which way. Jakey stumbled and then Pfen was on top of a force, one that had thrown Jakey. In the center of the restaurant, a shape, lithe, yet muscular, strong and radiating power, was forming. The legs came first, as if a veil was being taken away. They were concealed in thick, black army boots, ones that hid other secrets too. The pants came next, deep black ones that shone in the sun. Kevin knew who this was. The studded jacket came next, a gun inside of the right sleeve. Then the face. The striking features, blonde hair, a small, yet chiseled face. This was the man. The one who had tried to kill Kevin.

"Hello, Kevin." The man's smile was warm, yet cold, and cruelty was behind it. Kevin ran for the only weapon he had, Pfen, but was stopped short by a clicking sound. He turned, to see two revolvers in the man's hands, black and deadly.

"Don't move, or you are dead." The man's words were timed and precise, as if he had rehearsed it. Kevin's arms were up, in surrender. Jakey, too. Then he said,

"Kevin I know what you're planning. You aren't allowed to fuse in public. The people will see, and we'll be hunted down for lab experiments and stuff." His crutches fell, and then the cashier was up, out of his unconsciousness.

"Well, what did I miss?"

Two gunshots. Two gunshots changed the man's life. Two gunshots killed him, and flew through the man's head, splattering blood over the counter. The man had turned for a split second, but that was all Kevin needed. He and Pfen were fusing already, turning into the great beast, Pfenoli. They were on top of the man, gnashing their teeth, and hitting, kicking, punching and hacking. Sadie and Jakey stepped forward, but Pfenoli roared as the man's bullets flew into him.

"Go!" the voice thundered. Sadie and Jakey ran, out of the store, and towards Companion Orphanage. The two forces, Pfenoli and the man rolled over a broken chair, Pfenoli snatching it up and slamming it on the man's head.

"I am Nikolei, nice to meet you. I will kill you." Nikolei sneered.

"It's not your place to say that!" Kevin roared.

"Yes, it is." The man's eyes fell back, and both guns went off, hitting Pfenoli in the chest. The wolf man stumbled out of the broken down place, already hearing sirens wailing across the street. Pfen and Kevin unformed, Kevin's arms shaking. He was close, close to CO, so close. Kevin hit the ground. He was shaking uncontrollably. His chest hurt. It was painful, throbbing and hurting him. His hand went to it, and when it came back, blood was smeared across his fingertips. His head was reeling. He had killed an evil man, but instead of feeling relieved, or rejoiceful he felt empty. He keeled over, throwing up. The man might have been evil, but Kevin was horrified. He had killed someone. A human being. Kevin hadn't cared about Brechen. They were pure evil, but men, Kevin couldn't. He looked at his hands, horrified at what they had done. Kevin's eyes rolled into his head, and he fell onto the ground in Central park. Kevin laid there, a speck in the middle of a big city. As the police ran over him, heading for the fast food restaurant, Kevin was a bloody speck, lying in the middle…

21
Taking Action

KEVIN'S EYES FLICKERED open, his head throbbing as he found himself in the same room. His hand flew to his chest; the pain though, had faded to a dull feeling that hurt but was bearable. He remembered the details of yesterday, the man, the bullets, everything. He couldn't bear it. Killing someone. He looked at the calendar that he had tacked up before, when he had gone for a walk. It was August 12th, seven days after he had gone for the walk. Seven. Kevin had been in the hospital for seven days and he hadn't known it. As he stepped out of bed, Kevin winced in pain. His left arm hung limply by his side. His Mark was still on his arm, shining with the silver blue, and the black moon. Pfen lay at the end of the bed, his silvery eyes gazing watchfully at Kevin.

Sleep well?

I was fine really. Kevin replied, smiling at his companion.

Well, does it hurt?

Yeah, a lot.

The man,

I know.

No, you don't.

No, I do. I killed him. We killed him.

He's not dead. Far from it actually, I saw him run from the store, and he was in perfect condition.

Kevin's anger burned. *What else?*

He shot you again, but without a bullet. It looked more like a fang.

A fang?

A fang. Kevin's mind whirled as he tried to comprehend it. Then, the pieces were fitting, Kevin knew everything, and before he announced it to Pfen, someone was at the door.

"Who is it?" Kevin asked.

"Darren." Kevin whirled around to see his friend in khaki shorts, with endless pockets. He wore a white shirt, and his old sunglasses. And a pair of sandals. His blades were strapped to his side. Kevin still wondered something, something that he thought had been answered, yet it didn't make sense.

"Darren, come on in." he waved a hand to Darren, and they made their way to a second room, with a video game console and four seats, a controller on each one.

"Darren." His friend turned around towards him.

"Yeah?" Darren asked, his shaded glasses giving away nothing.

"When I first met you, you told me your nickname, Outcast of the Seas. When you told me the story, it didn't quite explain it. It told me nothing to tell me you were an outcast. Can you explain your name, please?" Darren sighed, and swallowed.

"Okay, but you have to promise that you'll keep this a secret, just between the two of us." Kevin nodded.

"Alright. You know the man I told you about, Old Joe?" Kevin nodded.

"Well, he was the true Outcast, but when he died, he gave me something. Something to pass on. You see, there was a legacy, and without knowing, I was thrown into it. I became the Outcast, not by choice, but because he passed it on. The Outcast, is hated by all of the creatures of the sea, but the Outcast, he can do something special." Darren sighed. "Why am I telling you this anyways? I shouldn't, I really shouldn't."

"Darren, you can trust me."

"I know that, but will you believe me?"

"Animals can speak, freaky monsters trying to kill me, I really don't see what I *can't* believe right now."

"Good point. Okay. I am a special Outcast, one that is called a Water Wielder. I can manipulate water to do what I like." Kevin's jaw dropped slightly.

"Can I see?" Darren rolled his eyes and turned on the faucet. He stretched out his arm, and the water kept running.

"Darren. Are you okay?" Darren shushed Kevin, who turned his head to the water. His jaw dropped again. There, in front of him, the water had taken a form. Mist swirled around it, curling around. Inside of the faucet was a soldier, about two feet tall. The water made him appear a transparent, light blue color, mini blades sheathed inside. The marble sink was already coming off, curling on the edges, and being drawn to the little figure. First the sword, stuck together by marble became solid, hard and cold in the water person's grasp. Then the legs, turned to marble, its cream color crawling up them as if the marble itself were liquid. The soldier was now all marble, the water transfixed inside. Darren picked up the soldier, and held it out to Kevin.

"It's a Sherken." Kevin took it.

"A shiruken? Isn't that a type of throwing star?"

"No, a Sherken, a mini man. They fight by your side until death. I just made you a Sherken."

"Oh. I think I get it." Darren nodded and they picked up their controllers.

"Let's just play. No words, my head hurts." Darren didn't object to that.

After a couple of hours, Darren left. Kevin made his way to his bed, releasing a breath. Ms. Shard stepped in, carrying a tray. On it was a sandwich, a bag of potato chips and orange juice.

"Thank you." Kevin said.

"You're welcome." She began to walk away, but Kevin asked her a question,

"Um, what happened to the place where I got shot?"

"Well, I can't talk too much…" she faded off, but Kevin pulled up his sleeve to show his Mark, and she spoke.

"Purget, you can come out." She said. A small, furry shape crawled over her shoulder, a long snout with small tufts inside of the ears. Tiny claws, and a long tail sprouted from it.

"What is it?" Kevin asked.

"He's, well, Purget is a hybrid," she said.

"After my mother and father died, CO took me in, and I became a nurse. Purget is my only connection to my family I have."

"What happened to the food place?" Kevin asked.

"It was destroyed in a fire. Everyone knows that the man who shot you did it; it's just a matter of time before he's found. The cashier was found with two bullets in his head and the fire was tamed shortly after."

"Thanks." She nodded and walked off. As Kevin's eyes fluttered closed, he knew what, or who had killed his parents.

The hall of the hospital was desolate. Night had taken over. An eerie stillness crept among the shadows and drifted through. Until an unknown force penetrated the veil of quiet. A small form crept from room 92, and scurried towards the exit. Behind it, a shadow, barely noticeable moved behind the first shape. The boy made his way to an exit, and the door opened, then closed briefly. Kevin was dressed in casual attire, a navy blue shirt, black cargoes and heavy boots. As he drifted through the passageways of CO, Kevin's mind wandered. He slid through a large door marked: "WEAPONS". As the light switch flipped, Kevin couldn't help but marvel at the racks of weapons, ranging from an automatic machine gun to an old sling with a pouch of stones. He slipped on a belt, with two long and thick pieces of worn leather that went over his shoulders and made an X on his back and two vertical lines from his chest to waist. He selected a long knife, a Scottish dirk, weighed it in his hands and sheathed it in a spot on his belt to his right. He had something else to retrieve for his left side. Kevin made his way to the corner marked: "FIREARMS", and selected two pistols with long muzzles. He pocketed them inside of two holsters on the vertical lines, and moved on. He picked up a shotgun and weighed it in his hand, but he dropped it, not liking the weight. He looked to the other corner, and checked the label. It read: "RUACH ENHANCED". Kevin had no idea what that meant. Kevin walked over along the shelf of the firearms and picked up two stun grenades. He grabbed a camo satchel, and stuffed the grenades inside. Along with those, he pocketed a knife, the charred piece of wood and his flashlight. He didn't understand why he took the piece of wood, just that he wanted it. He noticed a glimmer in the center of the room and walked forward. It was the RUACH ENHANCED section. He found nothing. He saw another glimmer and whirled around. In the back of the room, a painting was displayed. It was of a pedestal, and mounted on the pedestal was The Scepter of David. Kevin thought back rapidly to when he had first been here. There hadn't been a painting. He looked back at the picture. It looked so real. He stepped towards it and pressed his hand to the wall, though when he did, it was not a wall, but a new chamber. Kevin stepped in and took the Scepter into his hands. A surge of warmth rocketed into him and he sheathed it on his left side.

"Desperate times call for desperate measures." Kevin muttered. He left the room, and he and Pfen didn't notice a different person enter the room.

Can we find it? Kevin asked Pfen as they made their way towards the center of CO, the cafeteria. Sadie had told him that they weren't eating there because of the pit, so he targeted there first. Old habits kicked in, and Kevin took the shortcut that he and Jakey took on their way to lunch. It was their way, sneaking through secret passageways and such. Kevin went around a bend. Immediately, he turned to face the wall and his hands drifted over the portrait of a lion. In the far left corner, a small bush was out of place, turned upside down, and Kevin twisted it so that it was right way up. He poked it, and it fell back to reveal a doorway. If he was correct, it would lead them to the basement part of the cafeteria which was the pit, and he the basement of the cafeteria, which was th pit, and he and Pfen had seen an opening while running. He stepped in and sealed the door shut. He ran, but soon stopped, for his chest was hurting. As he stopped to take a breath, he heard the low thudding of footsteps.

Someone's here, he said to Pfen.

Let's move then. They stumbled along the path, Kevin glancing back into the darkness, still hearing the pounding of footsteps.

"Kevin!" a voice shouted, penetrating the eerie thudding. Kevin swerved around into the face of Darren. He was wearing an orange sweater, with loose jeans and white converses. His gleaming golden swords were strapped on his waistband. He was out of breath and sweat had matted his hair onto his head.

"Darren?" Kevin asked in disbelief.

"The same." Kevin smiled, and they trudged on, quietly conversing as they went.

"So how did you find me?" Kevin asked.

"Heard you sneaking out of your room. I'm never asleep, so when I heard you, it was deafening."

"I was that loud?"

"Yeah, but I think the silence had something to do with it."

"Oh, okay." Kevin motioned to continue.

"I saw you go into the weapons room, and I waited for you to leave. Then, I went in and got my blades." Kevin nodded, understanding so far. "Then, I saw you come here, and I knew where you were going." Darren finished.

"And you're here to stop me from going?" Kevin asked.

"No, I'm here to make sure that you don't kill yourself."

"Oh, I get it." Kevin said.

"This is pretty neat, these passageways and all," Darren said, motioning to the tunnel.

"Yeah, Jakey and I used to go around here and get to lunch faster than Sadie."

They both knew that they might not see Jakey or Sadie ever again, so they walked on in silence. As they neared the opening, the eerie bluish glow cast a forlorn shadow over the tunnel. Kevin put his finger to his lips, hearing a thunderous voice roaring through the halls, "He has forgotten us! I'm gonna kill him when this is over! Kill him!" Epharlan thundered.

"Anger issues," Darren tutted. Kevin turned to him and Darren asked,

"What?"

"Tell you if we live," Kevin mouthed. They crept towards the opening and slid out, Kevin, then Darren. Kevin's hand went to his pistols as Epharlan sniffed the air. In the center of the cavern, the hulking shapes of Epharlan and Spargatus loomed over the half eaten skeleton of a moose. Darren drew his blades.

"Sorry to spoil the party." He nodded to Kevin and two pops echoed through the room as the bullets were buried in each monster's forehead. Kevin flew back and dropped his guns. He rubbed his arm and snatched up his pistol. He turned to see the two monsters. Spargatus recoiled and screeched, while Epharlan grunted in anger.

"Hey, I know you," Epharlan growled, his beady eyes fixing on Kevin.

"Yeah, and soon, you're going to know me!" shouted Darren. He jumped from his perch about ten feet high and landed on Epharlan's back, hacking away with his blades. Kevin had hopped to the ground and fired three bullets. The recoil threw him back and his hand snapped back. He dropped the gun, but quickly recovered it. *Twice Kevin! Twice!* His mind screamed. *Be ready next time!* Kevin stood up and saw where the bullets had hit. Spargatus had roared as each one sunk into him, one into his hand, one into his end, and one into his right eye. His left eye turned to Kevin, fury raging in it. The other was red rimmed, blood pouring from the fresh wound. His scales began to change, turning darker, from transparent to blue, to purple, to black. As the color spread from bottom up, each bullet popped out harmlessly onto the ground. The flood of color stopped at the neck, though and instead of becoming black, the head became a furious red, boiling over with anger. Kevin gasped and backed up, scrambling to reload his gun. He had put one away and the other was in his hand. Spargatus's tail struck quickly, throwing the gun out of his hand, making the gun slide across the ground, yards from Kevin. He cursed and then dove for the pistol, Spargatus lunging after him. The snake was in the air, claws splayed out mouth showing those hideous, purple fangs and Kevin picked up his gun, scrambling for the trigger. He fired, once twice, three times. Kevin smiled, but his smile disappeared as each bullet bounced harmlessly off of Spargatus and fell onto Kevin, charred and smoking. Before he could comprehend, Spargatus was on Kevin, a mix of claws and teeth and venom, sizzling and popping. His hand came up, ready for the killing blow, but then he felt a sharp, twisting pain in his head. His good eye rolled up to see Pfen, growling and biting as his teeth tore into the only exposed part of Spargatus: his head. The snake writhed in pain, his hands scrabbling for the wolf. It gave Kevin time. His hand drifted over the Scepter, and it was a sword, ready for action. He didn't have time to marvel, but he made a mental note that if he survived, he would look into the amazing weapon. His blade whirred through the air as he sliced Spargatus. His cheek had a long gash, but he didn't care. It sank into the black scales and Kevin ran at the monster, slicing and hacking at it. Pfen jumped into Kevin, but he didn't feel it, all he felt was a rush of wind. With Pfen, their blade rushed through the air. Pfenoli smiled. Spargatus' face contorted in fear, and the blade struck, cleanly cleaving the head off. The head, though, was staring at him in a lopsided grin. It was disgusting. The body flopped to the ground, and began to dissolve into a pool of silvery blue. Kevin looked back to Darren. Epharlan had fared as Spargatus, and was already melting. His eyes focused on something else, a blood-soaked figure lying on the ground.

"DARREN!"

Four weeks later

Kevin's eyes fluttered open. His head throbbed and his cheek still burned, but all in all, he was fine. He looked down at Pfen, on his feet. The wolf, now just about full-grown was about three and a half feet tall, his pelt shaggy, covering a thick, muscular frame. Kevin smiled. Pfen looked exactly like Pfenolus, his father. He patted his companion and stretched his legs, then arms and hopped out of bed. He scratched his head and moved to the bathroom, where he took a shower, prepared, and got dressed. He stepped out, wearing a blue and white striped Polo t-shirt with black jeans and sneakers.

"Come on Pfen." They stepped out, Kevin locking his room door shut as he walked to Jakey's room. He pounded on the door, and heard the thumping of feet, a muffled voice and then a loud, jarring thud. Kevin raised his eyebrow and the door opened to reveal his friend Jakey, who most likely had just thrown on his outfit. It was a dark blue hoodie, with black sweatpants and Nikes. Jakey's companion, Howlin, ruffled his feathers then hopped onto Pfen. The two animals conversed a little then looked up at Kevin and Jakey. Jakey grinned wolfishly at Kevin then asked,

"Ready?"

"You bet." They made their way to the bottom floor and to a room marked: DARREN H. Kevin knocked and a voice said,

"Come in." They opened the door but didn't step in. In front of them, water stretched endlessly throughout the room. A bed floated aimlessly around the pool, and in the right corner, was about an eight-foot square of solid ground in each corner, containing a drawer and some seats. Kevin looked down into the water.

"Darren, I know you're in there," he said, looking down into the depths. He saw a dart in the water, then another, and then another. Then he saw a blob, getting bigger and bigger. Kevin stepped back. "Jakey!" a seven-foot long leatherback turtle shot from the water, a blonde haired boy latching onto its back. Jakey, unfortunately too close was thrown into the water.

"Pahh- ptoo! Help! I can't swim! I can't swim!" he wailed, his hands floundering, yet his feet kicking precisely enough so it looked like he was drowning, yet really wasn't. Darren wheeled Hawksbeak around so that he could reach out his hand to lift Jakey up. Jakey accepted it but lurched back and pulled Darren under. Jakey and Darren wrestled in the water, each one pulling the other under for a while until Kevin reminded them, "We've got to beat Sadie to breakfast."

Jakey floundered for a moment then exclaimed, "We're just having a bit of fun."

Kevin's expression didn't change. "Alright," Jakey said, sliding out of the water, "We'll just dry up." They walked over to a large vent in the wall and Darren pressed a button. Warm air launched out of it, drying both boys except their hair. Darren was wearing his regular attire, a beach button up, cargo shorts and sandals with sunglasses. He smirked and Kevin noticed the gruesome mark that Epharlan had left behind. A scar, starting from the side of his head, arced down his body and made its way to his left ankle. When Darren smiled, it twisted so that the scar made a sort of dimple on his cheek. The pair walked towards him, grinning devilishly.

"What's going on?" Kevin asked. Their hands were behind their backs.

"Happy birthday!" Their hands shot out and threw Kevin into the water. He yelled and plunged in, surfacing for breath. He gasped and swam to the edge where the dryer was. He clicked the button and was blasted by warm air. He remembered this day. This was his birthday. It was also the day his parents had died. He laughed slightly, clearing tears from his eyes.

"Kevin?" Jakey asked, "We have your presents, I- is anything wrong?"

Kevin shook his head, "No, it's just, they, they died one year ago."

"Oh. Okay." There was a moment of silence, then Jakey motioned to Kevin and they walked out of the room. Darren walked up behind Kevin.

"You wanna go pay your respects?" he asked. Kevin nodded. They walked to the secret passage, and raced through, making it to the end of the tunnel within seconds. The clearing was now a place where Kevin and the gang hung out, but the old feeling of evil was still there. It lingered, even when its source didn't. In the center of the large cavern was a large table, decorated with fine works of art. Ms. Prince had had that made. Kevin, Jakey and Darren, along with their companions (minus Hawksbeak) walked down (Howlin glided) into the room. It was much more brightly lit and red banners adorned the old tunnels that had been blocked, while wooden and real weapons (old and modern) hung on racks. Kevin reached the bottom of the stairs and ran towards his shelf, one with wooden and real weapons alike. He turned to his friends, and they produced large boxes, wrapped with paper and bows.

"Forget me?" a voice called from the top stair. Kevin looked up to find Sadie, in casual attire. She wore a pink blouse with jean shorts cut just above her knees and her hair was tied back in a ponytail. Kevin greeted her and Jakey bowed, receiving a punch in the stomach.

"Hey! What was that for?" he whispered to Kevin. Sadie turned and raised an eyebrow. Jakey hushed himself.

"Happy birthday, Kev," Darren said, handing him a blue box tied with golden ribbon. Kevin tore it open to reveal a video game, WW II Secret services.

"Thanks Darren." Kevin set it on a leather couch that was leaned against the stairs. Sadie handed him a red box with little HBs on it, which Kevin thought meant "happy birthday." He opened it to reveal a watch with little wires and gizmos sticking out.

"Sadie, what is it?"

"What you have there is your own little watch grenade. You see?" She said.

Kevin dropped it.

"Careful. You could break it."

"Why- why are you giving me a bomb on my birthday?" Kevin asked.

"Correction, grenade. Just in case you need it. And to activate it, you click that little button right there," she said, pointing to a small square button with gold print that Kevin had to squint to read: "DETONATE."

"And, how do I stop myself from getting killed by using this?" Kevin asked.

"You see the time handle? Well you choose an amount of time for it to go off in and click detonate. It does seconds, minutes and hours. I'll give you the instruction manual in a sec. And by the way," she said with a sly smile, "It tells perfect time." She tossed him a small packet and Kevin caught it deftly, shoving it in his back pocket. He made a mental note never to sleep with it. He buckled it on and Jakey shoved a box into his hands. It was wrapped in green paper with plastic casing on the edges. Kevin peeled it and opened it to reveal another box, this one red. He ripped it again, to reveal a blue wrapping reading Happy B-day! Kevin looked up at Jakey in frustration. Jakey nodded with anticipation. Kevin ripped it again. This one was gold, reading Merry Christmas! Kevin slapped his forehead in exasperation and continued on.

Thirty-six un-wrappings later

Wrapping paper littered the floor at Kevin's feet. He looked at his present from Jakey. It was actually a small, cardboard box with a blue coating of paint. He opened it, closing his eyes, expecting another box, but there was none, just a shimmering blade in the center. It was purple, the same color as Spargatus's teeth. The edges were serrated and made of gold, gleaming like the sun. The hilt was black as night, a deep red ruby shining in the middle. Even though it looked sharp, the handle was surprisingly comfortable in Kevin's hand and gave him a warm sensation throughout his body. Kevin felt giddy inside. In golden letters, close to the handle it was inscribed: "FLAME CHARGE". Kevin looked at Jakey and grinned.

"You wanna know where I got it?" he asked. Kevin nodded, his gaze unwavering as he looked at the blade.

"It was from Spargatus' remains, I found it and wanted to give it to you." Kevin's jaw dropped. Jakey's hands flew in the air, "Before you start cursing me, turn it over!" he exclaimed. Kevin flipped the blade over and it read:

"What's it supposed to mean?" Kevin asked.

"Flip it over again." Kevin turned it so that the blade was facing downwards. The print now read:

"Oh, I see why you got it." Kevin remarked. Jakey nodded, smiling, "Yeah." Kevin put it in its case and began to walk steadily up the staircase.

"What're you doing?" Jakey asked him.

"Paying my respects."

Kevin looked down at the two bleak gravestones, wiping tears away. He dropped the flowers, purple flowers. He didn't know what they were, but he knew his mother had liked them, so he brought them. In the middle of their graves, and his fingers lightly grazed the looming holes in his life. He knew he would never see them again, never feel his mother's sweet kiss on the forehead, never experience his father's embrace ever again. Kevin knew, yet didn't want it to be true. It couldn't be, but it was, and the two most important things in his life were gone, taken by death's grasp. Kevin splayed out his hands on each stone. He blinked back tears, but one streaked down his cheek. Kevin looked at Pfen beside him, the only thing he had close to family. But there was Jakey and Darren and Sadie. They had been his family since they had met and even now stood faithfully by his side. He promised himself to cherish them, to hold them forever. His hands shuffled through his pockets, finding his flashlight, which he could never part with for some reason, his knife, Flame Charge, and the charred piece of wood. The Scepter of David hung limply by his side, forgotten by Kevin, who had been seized by grief. Kevin looked back up at his parents' gravestones.

"Kevin." He whirled around, not expecting the voice. Darren stepped

"Darren, I had thought that you were Nik-" *Nikolei*, it hung in the air, a bad omen to Kevin, and a forsaken word.

"Yes. I understand."

"You do?" Kevin asked. Darren nodded.

"Yes, I do, Kevin Buckheimer."

"How do you know my last name? I never told you it. How do you know my last name?"

"I know everything, Kevin. I was there, when your parents died. I killed them. A simple accident by leaving the stove on with a box of oil, then a couple cigarettes on the ground and it was easy." Kevin's face was a mix of hatred and fury.

"Darren, you?"

"No, sadly, Darren has been locked up for a while, don't you see? I am not Darren." He said, pointing to his cheek where there was no scar.

"Nikolei." Kevin breathed. Darren's face began to droop and sag, contorting into different shapes, and soon, instead of a child, there was Nikolei, the man who had killed Kevin's parents, and later had tried to kill Kevin. He drew a gun, and pointed it at Kevin, smiling evilly.

"I knew that you were tricky, getting away three times, three. But now, now I have you." Kevin put the pieces together.

"You- you didn't want to kill my parents, you wanted to kill me." Kevin croaked.

"Yes, you see, my master had a hunch about you, and it proves he was correct," Nikolei said, nodding towards Kevin's right arm. Kevin looked at him.

"My parents died because you were trying to kill me, yet you failed."

"You see, I was your true enemy, not Spargatus. I am the one who had Spargatus bite you on your arm in the very spot in case you survived the fire, in case I needed to track you down. Now, after I'm done with you, I can move on to your precious friends, and the orphanage." Nikolei said, pointing to the two fang marks on Kevin's arm.

"The nip at the fire," Kevin breathed. He looked up at Nikolei. "You, you, Nikolei killed my parents."

"Alas, not Nikolei." He said, growing taller and more menacing, his face becoming a snout, and two, purple fangs flicking from a red-scaled head, two long, tree-like arms sprouting from a winding snake body as thick as a grown man head to toe.

"S-S-Spargatus isss my real name. It was me, the entire time, pulling the strings behind the scenes. Nikolei was just too much of an idiot to understand. Those Extincts can't control us. We are too powerful." The snake said, hissing at Kevin. "Now, give me your tasty blood, Orphan Leader!"

"I won't let you." The snake hissed mockingly at him, and raised a hand to slam onto Kevin.

"I won't let you touch my friends!" Kevin looked up, his eyes black, and long, thin veins stretching out from beneath him.

"Not ever!" He caught Spargatus's hand, and threw him into a gravestone.

Kevin roared at Spargatus, and rushed forward, his blade whirring as he sliced at the menacing evil. The snake reared back, and deftly threw the blade aside, sending the sword crashing to the ground. Pfen covered him as Kevin stopped for a moment, and with one sweep of Spargatus's arm, was thrown into a gravestone, and crumple to the ground, immobilized. Kevin screamed, and pulled a blade out of his pocket, resorting to it last. He rushed forward, slicing the snake where its stomach should be. It screeched in pain and clutched its stomach, burning fire crackling up the side of his body.

"Flame Charge." Kevin said, understanding its namesake. He dropped it and dove for his sword, rolling around and rushing at it. Flame Charge was the last thing he wanted to use. Kevin's blade sliced down, and the snake's side erupting blue blood, simply oozing from its cracks. Slightly silver blue blood squirted over Kevin's face. Then the snake's form changed, and it was Nikolei, and he was holding a gun.

"I won't let you touch them. They gave me a home. They made me feel like I had a family again," He looked back at Sadie, and smiled, his black eyes and veins fading.

"So I won't let you hurt them! Not ever! This is my home, and as long as I'm here, you won't ever get to them!"

Kevin braced for the impact of a bullet, but the only impact was a rush of wind. Pfenoli charged Spargatus, sword in hand. Man changed to snake, and Spargatus matched them, his claws shining black as night. Pfenoli twisted around, and the blade fell from their hands, clattering onto the ground next to the gravestone of Kevin's mother. They dove for one thing, their last resort. Snatching it up, Kevin hurled the knife Flame Charge at Spargatus, and it buried itself in its chest, a little under, right in the heart. The snake looked down in disbelief. Pfenoli walked forward, fetching their sword.

"Don't ever threaten my friends again. Ever."

"Wait! I'm not the only one who took part in killing your parents, do not shed innocent blood." Kevin scowled, and the sword reared up, and arced down, the snake's head sliding off like a knife through butter.

"Goodbye." Kevin looked at Pfen, who was in a crumple on the ground, and looked back at the snake. It was Nikolei, and even without his head, the gun was pointed at Kevin. Kevin picked the piece of wood from his pocket, and looked at it, before setting it down. This, he now knew why he had held onto it. It was him. This piece of wood, scarred by fire, isolated from the rest, hurt inside was him. He set it down in the bed of flowers. Someone whistled. Kevin turned around. It was the headless Nikolei, and the last thing Kevin heard, was *Pop!*

"Kevin!" Jakey screamed.

Kevin looked around, darkness and bleakness shrouding his sight. Everywhere he looked, he saw swirling mist, coiled and slithering about. He looked in front of him, and saw a figure in shambles, shuffling in a line that spiraled downwards, a faint red glow burning there. Kevin looked behind him, and saw a man, slivers of skin peeled off of his face.

"Where am I?" Kevin asked quietly.

"Hell." The man croaked, his voice itchy as if he were still swallowing a large hunk of food. Kevin looked around. This definitely fit the description Kevin would have thought of!

"How? I'm not dead, I'm-" the man pointed at Kevin's chest. Kevin looked down. His shirt was in pieces, and under his shirt, blood stuck to him, matting everything. His hands pried through, feeling for where he had been hit, and he felt no pain. His hands glided over a rift, a small hole and he looked at it. It was small, but Kevin could see three more. He grimaced at himself, and looked back up at the man in disbelief.

"How?" Kevin asked. The man shrugged.

"It looks like you got shot."

"I know that." Kevin snapped, "But how am I dead?"

"Listen kid, you're dead. You're dead. The sooner you realize it, the sooner you feel it." The man looked back up, and didn't speak anymore. *You're dead.* The words echoed through his mind, growing larger as they crept through every part of his body, making him shudder. *You're dead.* Kevin grimaced and looked forward. He was next. The clearing was small, only enough for a couple people to squeeze into. There were two doorways in addition to the one Kevin had entered through, one leading to a beautiful golden corridor with a thin shroud over it, and another, a boiling stream of lava, swirling and bubbling as it meandered by. Kevin looked at the center of the room, where there was a chair, and in it was sitting a thin, and wiry man, two small wings peeking over his shoulders. Two gray eyes flitted behind large spectacles, reading a long scroll that curled around his legs and was splayed across the ground at the same time.

"Name?" he had a slight British accent, and his golden hair waved as he spoke.

"Kevin Buckheimer." Kevin replied, the words tasting bitter in his mouth.

"Just a moment." The angel bustled around, muttering slightly as he whirred through the pages, his hands a blur and his words even blurrier.

"Nope, no Kevin Blackturner, sorry, but you're not dead yet."

Not dead? Kevin turned around awkwardly, perspiration running down the sides of his head in beads. He walked away, and the man with peeled skin smiled at him, revealing black, and rotting teeth. Kevin nodded, and as he walked away, Kevin could hear his screams echo, as the lava river boiled him alive. He didn't look back. Kevin walked towards a light, and kept walking, and then he was in the front of it. His hand met it and a blinding flash of light illuminated the room. Kevin closed his eyes. When he didn't feel the burning sensation of the light, Kevin opened his eyes.

"Kevin!" three pairs of hands grasped him firmly into a hug. Kevin stared into the faces of Sadie, Jakey and Darren. He threw his head back and laughed aloud, and smiled. Kevin was alive.

22
Hero

KEVIN'S HAND SLAPPED yet another hand, and now, it was sore. He saw another kid walk up, and instead of slapping high five, he fist bumped. Pfen behind him said, *Hurry, I want to go and have some breakfast.*

Gotcha. They walked on, and when a high five, or fist bump was offered, he quickly returned it and moved on. He made it to the picture of the lion and twisted the bush, entering the secret passage. He locked it behind him and moved on, already hearing the voices in the distance. His chest hurt, but it was a dull pain, and he couldn't stand it. It was as if he was itching in one place, but when he went to scratch it, it would disappear. Kevin decided to leave the wounds alone, and let them heal. He made it to the clearing. It felt fresher, as if a storm cloud had been cleared, and now the sun was shining. Kevin looked down to see Jakey and Darren tussling, trading punches and slaps.

"You know better than that." Kevin said loudly, so that it echoed through the hall. They scrambled off of each other and dusted themselves off. Kevin rushed down and greeted them, Sadie, Darren and Jakey. They traded hugs and made it to another staircase on the opposite side of the cavern. They made their way up, and found a black door, which they couldn't see from the bottom, but it was easy to see from the top. Jakey twisted the knob and they went in, following the winding path. Kevin, Sadie, Jakey and Darren stepped into a bustling crowd of orphans, hungry, and ready to eat breakfast. As they settled down to eat, Kevin heard Ms. Prince walking up to the podium and beginning a speech.

"Children of CO, I am here to tell you, that without a certain student, we wouldn't have an orphanage to live in right now. Without him and his friends, we would be subject to the torment of Spargatus, Nikolei and Epharlan. So I want you to clap for," she said, beckoning for Sadie, Jakey and Darren to stand up, "Sadie, Jakey, and Darren!" an uproar of approval erupted from the rows of orphans as they cheered to the three children.

Kevin looked up and smiled at his friends. They sat down and grinned at him.

"And now, to the hero of it all, Kevin Buckheimer!" Kevin stood up, smiling inside and outside of him.

"Hero! Hero! Hero!" the students chanted. Kevin smiled, and thought to himself, *I'm a hero! I'm a hero!* And it's true. He was a hero.

23
Leader

KEVIN BUCKHEIMER STRODE through the dimly-lit hallways of Companion Orphanage, glancing around at admirers and accepting high fives from those who held out their hands. He made his way to the room marked "LISTENER" and slid inside. The room was empty.

"Ms. Prince? You in here?" he called out. There was no reply. He walked to the one desk in the center of the room and sat down, Pfen obediently lying by his side. Ms. Prince did that a lot, disappearing instead of staying in class. Kevin didn't mind, so he usually toyed with his Scepter of David that he brought everywhere. It was always buckled on his belt by his side and when he went to sleep, he kept it under his pillow. He glanced around the room and it looked somehow different, as if there was a stray piece of chalk, or a missing pencil. Yeah, Ms. Prince was that neat. He stood up and saw it; a board sticking up out of the ground, and under it was a deep pit, an abyss of black. He stepped forward, his grip on the opal that turned scepter to sword and looked down.

"Kevin," a wispy voice whispered like clear air into his ears.

"Who are you?" he said, snapping his scepter into a sword. Pfen stood up abruptly and walked to him.

What was that? Pfen asked.

Not sure, should we check it out?

Uh, yeah, let's do it. They hopped into the pit, Kevin then Pfen. The loose board, their only way out, shut, and the voice spoke again mockingly to Kevin.

"Lost your way, Listener?" it hissed.

"Show yourself." Kevin ordered. A light lit up in the right corner of the room, revealing a stone seat. On it sat a marble angel, wearing a flowing gold cloak and shining sapphire wings sprouting behind it.

"I am here." The stone angel said, it's voice crackling like thunder. Kevin's face turned from fierce to a mix of disbelief and bewilderment.

"I am the Oracle of the Most High. Listen to me, and heed my words."

"Kevin." He turned and saw Ms. Prince, a grave look spread throughout her bony features.

"What's going on?"

"This is the Oracle of the Most High, listen and then we will talk."

The marble angel slammed its fist into the bare rock wall. Pounds of old stone crumbled from it, like a small waterfall, spraying dust across the ground. It stretched its marble hand into a now gaping hole and retrieved a small scroll and began to read:

"The Prophecy Of The Leaders

Eight parentless shall come together,

To break the bonds of the evil tether

To show my Creation what is good and right

And give their opposer a great fright

The leader of the pack,

Brethren of the Great Wolf at his back,

Shall bestow the gift of an Orphan Leader,

To seven to build his army and take up arms against the enemy.

Bound to squabble until a beast unites their cause,

And breaks down all of their known barriers and laws.

But the message given upon these eight,

"Though death is near, live and love life to make it great!"

The battle won from a human loss

Who dies to defeat the Extinct's boss

This is The Prophecy Of The Leaders

For where these eight go, be humble greeters

The God of all"

The Oracle finished and handed the scroll to Kevin, and then it returned to its seat and its original form, stone again and a statue. Kevin looked up at Ms. Prince.

"My questing days are over. I'm in no way of going through this type of thing again," Ms. Prince shook her head, and said,

"What questing days? You were on no quest while hunting Spargatus. That wasn't a quest; simply a hunt where you were driven by revenge. Spargatus wanted this to happen, but you killed him and lived which wasn't what he planned. Spargatus toyed with you to go on this mad expedition. He played you, he played tricks on you. He lied to you in the body of Darren. Darren was his slave. Darren was locked up in a back corner because of Spargatus. No, Kevin, your questing days have just begun. You are the leader of the prophecy, you shall lead the other seven to their destiny. You are not done with this life Kevin. You are just beginning it. And that," Ms. Prince said, "Do you want to know what it is?" Kevin looked at the frozen angel and the scroll. Ms. Prince pulled a bundle from behind her back, and then Kevin asked, holding up the scroll,

"What is it?"

She smiled.

"It's your destiny, Kevin."

"My destiny." Kevin breathed.

Acknowledgments

Thank you God, for guiding me through every step of this book. Thank you Mom, for believing I could do it when no one else did. Thank you, Rebbecca for proofreading, and helping me to correct this book. And thank you, too Kadin. You're one of the best helps in the entire world. This book goes to Nikki, who died of cancer. No matter what, this book is the first, and I hope to make more and more. To my readers,

Mercy, peace and love be yours in abundance. Jude 1:2

Elijah F. Johnson, 2010

LOOK OUT FOR THE NEXT BOOK IN THE ORPHAN LEADERS SERIES:

THE BEAST

Kevin Buckheimer is back, and better than ever. When the children of C.O. leave for a trip to an island, a new threat, The Beast, threatens to take over the Preservatives and bring the world crashing down. Can Kevin, Jakey, Sadie and Darren stop this threat, or will the world be at the mercy of this terrifying creature's hands?

Find out in "the Beast"

General Morgan saw the creature coming at his force, full on. He shouted a command and his men, stopped from facing the wild wolf, turned to their oncoming foe. They gulped. But the general knew that they could do it. There were about one hundred fighting men here, and if he called for back up, he would have about one hundred seventy-five. He blew his whistle for reinforcement, just to be safe, and when they hadn't come in about a minute, he knew that his back up was dead. And so was he.

Saliva slathered at the edges of the mouth of the monster. A sleek, wolf like face arose, sprouting jagged, bloodstained teeth. Furious red eyes, rimmed with blood and red on the inside, shaded by black could kill someone with a stare. Its chest was broad, with gray, ragged fur that shot out in every which direction. Some was spiky, some matted with perspiration and blood. Its arms were longer than its legs, the same matted hair sticking across them. Three claws sprouted from the front of each, red on the ends of each. Its back legs were scaly with a gray tinge to them. Its tail sprouted about five feet long, and its height was monumental. It rushed head on at the force, its saliva turning red.

General Morgan saw it…

THE BEAST

Coming soon...

www.ingramcontent.com/pod-product-compliance
Lightning Source LLC
Chambersburg PA
CBHW070827250626
47170CB00006B/2234